**The dog hopped out of the truck
as soon as Jake opened the door and
followed close at his heels when he went back
to check on the horses. He'd just opened the
back gate of the trailer when she burst into
a ferocious round of barking.**

"Quiet," he shouted over the keening wind.

She barked even louder, her attention riveted on the dressing-room door at the front of the trailer.

"What, did we pick up a mouse at the last barn?" He unlocked the door and reached inside to flip on the lights, hoping it wasn't something larger than a mouse. The last thing he needed was to find that a barn cat had hitched a ride away from that last horse farm.

But it wasn't a barn cat staring at him from the far corner with wide hazel eyes, tousled auburn hair peeking out from beneath a knitted hat and pale skin turning blue with cold. It was a woman huddled in a pile of horse blankets, her teeth chattering and hands trembling.

And she had his rifle pointed straight at his chest.

Books by Roxanne Rustand

Love Inspired Suspense

*Hard Evidence
*Vendetta
*Wildfire
Deadly Competition
**Final Exposure
**Fatal Burn
**End Game
**Murder at Granite Falls
**Duty to Protect

†Aspen Creek Crossroads
*Snow Canyon Ranch
**Big Sky Secrets

Love Inspired

†Winter Reunion
†Second Chance Dad
The Loner's Thanksgiving
  Wish

ROXANNE RUSTAND

lives in the country with her husband and a menagerie of pets, many of whom find their way into her books. She works part-time as a registered dietitian at a psychiatric facility, but otherwise you'll find her writing at home in her jammies, surrounded by three dogs begging for treats, or out in the barn with the horses. Her favorite time of all is when her kids are home—though all three are now busy with college and jobs.

RT Book Reviews nominated her for a Career Achievement Award in 2005, and she won the magazine's award for Best Superromance of 2006.

She loves to hear from readers! Her snail-mail address is P.O. Box 2550, Cedar Rapids, Iowa, 52406-2550. You can also contact her at: www.roxannerustand.com, www.shoutlife.com/roxannerustand or at her blog, where readers and writers talk about their pets: www.roxannerustand.blogspot.com.

DUTY TO PROTECT

Roxanne Rustand

Love Inspired

Recycling programs for this product may not exist in your area.

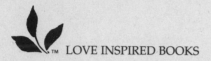

LOVE INSPIRED BOOKS

ISBN-13: 978-0-373-08289-6

DUTY TO PROTECT

Copyright © 2011 by Roxanne Rustand

www.LoveInspiredBooks.com

Printed in U.S.A.

Don't worry about anything; instead, pray about everything. Tell God what you need, and thank him for what he has done. If you do this, you will experience God's peace, which is far more wonderful than the human mind can understand. His peace will guard your hearts and minds as you live in Christ Jesus.
—*Philippians* 4:6–7

In loving memory of my mom, Arline.

ONE

The soft blanket of new snow glittered under the streetlamp and muffled her steps as Emma strode from the city bus stop at the end of the block to the side door of her garage. Anxiety twisted her stomach into a tight knot of fear.

The snow could muffle the sound of someone else's steps, too.

And even now, that unknown person could be watching her. Waiting. Just as he had waited for her father last week.

She'd been only a few feet away from her dad, pushing a cart of groceries in the busy Safeway parking lot. He'd suddenly faltered to a stop. "We've got to leave," he'd whispered urgently. "I just saw——"

Then he'd fallen face-first, a widening pool of crimson spreading through the slushy snow beneath him. He died at her feet, and she hadn't even heard the gunshot.

Had he seen his killer's face? Why hadn't the shooter taken her out, too? The melee of screaming frightened people running for cover would have given the shooter ample opportunity to pull the trigger, and he probably wouldn't have missed. From the perfect placement of the single bullet in her father's skull, the cops figured the killer possessed sniper experience.

Which meant the killer was someone sent by the drug cartel that had been trying to kill Emma and her adoptive family for years. Orphaned at the age of seven and taken in by an older, childless couple a year later, she'd longed for love and security in her new home but had found little of either.

And now even that connection to a family was gone.

Taking a slow breath, she willed away the horrific images of blood and panicking people, and willed her heartbeat to slow. *I'm okay. I'm almost home.*

She unlocked the door of the garage and slipped inside, then rounded the rear bumper of her old Blazer, thankful that the dark, smoke-tinted windows hid its contents. No one could look inside and guess at what she planned to do tomorrow—not that anyone was likely to drop by. No one ever did.

The Witness Protection Program was no place to make friends, and with luck, anyone who'd known her in her former life probably figured she was dead.

From somewhere inside the house came a thud. She paused, her hand on the door leading from the garage into the tiny entryway off the kitchen. That hadn't been the sound of the furnace kicking in. There was no one else who had a key. A crazy longing flitted through her thoughts. *It's just Dad—*

But he was dead and so was her mom, and now she was totally and forever alone. Surely she was just hearing things. She lowered her gaze to the doorknob, started to fit her key into the dead bolt.

But then she heard another thud. An anguished moan.

And were those *voices* inside? They came closer. Both male, both agitated.

She'd locked all the doors and armed the security system when she left. Not even her WITSEC contact knew its code—yet there were intruders inside. So where were the sirens? The squadron of patrol cars that should be closing in? Had the alarm even triggered?

Warning bells sounded in her head.

An inner voice screamed at her to run.

Rising on her tiptoes, she braced her trembling fingertips on the door frame for a quick glance through the window set high in the door. A narrow gap between

the loose-woven curtains on the inside re-
vealed just a slice of the kitchen, but the
bright lights inside illuminated more than
enough.

Horror and disbelief swept through
her as she stumbled away from the door,
caught herself and swallowed hard, trying
to hold back a wave of sudden nausea.

It couldn't be.

A body was lying facedown on her
kitchen floor, the hilt of her favorite carv-
ing knife rammed upright into his back.
The dark, wet pool of blood spreading
from beneath him was a shocking contrast
to the white tile floor.

She forced herself to take another quick
look.

A vaguely familiar cop hunkered down
next to the body, and a tall, dark-haired
stranger in a long black overcoat and
dove-gray slacks moved into view, facing
away from her. A detective, maybe?

A rush of relief swept through her. The
cops *were* already here. Everything would

be all right. But just as quickly, she knew this scene was all wrong.

The cop's face was dark red with anger, and sweat beaded his forehead. "You shouldn'ta done it," he bellowed.

The other man gestured at the body. "He was a loose cannon, you fool. I had *orders*."

"Yeah. But—"

"Okay. So we'll do the woman with his gun. Get the angle right and the investigators will think she stabbed him, then he managed to turn and fire in self-defense before he went down."

The cop swore, low and fierce. "Opportunity. Means. But just *try* and give me a plausible motive."

"Her dad's murder. She…figured Todd blew their cover."

"So a mousy little librarian was able to kill a guy this size? With his self-defense training? Tell me another one."

"We've got time. We can fix this scene—

make it look right. No one will ever know different."

The rising argument between the two men faded away as the walls of the garage started to spin. Todd? Todd Hlavicek?

She wobbled away from the door, her heart in her throat and her knees quivering as she half fell against the front fender of the Blazer.

Todd was her only current contact in the Witness Protection Program. He was the *only* one in the area who should have known about her adoptive family's involvement in the WITSEC program and their whereabouts...yet *loose cannon* implied that his loyalty had been bought.

Had he betrayed her family for money? Had he been coerced? Either way, the fact that he was dead reemphasized just how dangerous her family's old enemies were. How long they could hold a grudge.

She was the only one left, and she was going to be next.

She had to get out of here. But the

garage door was closed and the noise of rolling it up would rumble like thunder in this enclosed space, alerting the men inside. Trying to reach someplace safe on foot would be useless. This was a quiet neighborhood of large yards and inexpensive 1940s ramblers filled with people she didn't know. As always, she'd carefully avoided friendships with the neighbors. Whose life could she dare risk by begging for sanctuary?

The muffled argument inside the house stopped abruptly. Had they heard her?

Oh, Lord—please, please...

She whirled around, jerked open the SUV's door and threw herself inside, slamming her hand against the locks as she searched for the keys she'd dropped in her pocket.

Her fingers closed over them and she tried to push the key into the ignition. Fumbled. Tried again.

Please...please...*please*...

A scream threatened to tumble from her

lips when the kitchen door flew open and flooded the garage with light. The cop stood in the open doorway, his face a mask of anger, his right hand already reaching for the service revolver at his side.

With shaking fingers she tried the key again. Felt it slide home. The engine roared when she shoved the gearshift into Reverse and floored the accelerator. Tires squealed as the vehicle launched backward, splintering the flimsy garage door.

A deafening explosion enveloped her as the front windshield shattered and something hot whistled past her ear.

Throwing her weight against the pedal, she flicked a last glance at the two men racing after her. One grabbed at her car door but fell away as the SUV shimmied, nearly out of control. She swung it into a wild arc, over a trash can. She rammed the gearshift into Drive and again floored the accelerator. The SUV crossed an edge of the lawn and shot toward the highway.

Pop.

Pop.

Pop.

The sounds were distant. Toylike. Surreal—until the rear windshield shattered into a glittering network of crystalline fabric. They would be on her tail the minute they reached their vehicles.

She wasn't armed. She had no experience in high-speed driving. She had to make it two full blocks to the freeway ramp, and pray the Chicago rush hour traffic was still heavy. If she could disappear into that bumper-to-bumper mass of frustrated and impatient drivers before her pursuers caught up, she might have a chance to live until tomorrow.

God hadn't listened to many of her prayers over the years, far as she could tell, and she'd long-ago drifted away from the silent, one-way conversations she'd had with Him as a child. Yet He must have tuned into her pleas today.

She had no illusions about her odds of evading a determined cop with any number of high-speed chases under his belt. But she hadn't noticed a cruiser parked near her house and there hadn't been a civilian's car parked nearby, either, other than Todd's black Taurus sedan. If the other two had left their cars far enough away to avoid the curious eyes of neighbors, she could be in luck.

A patrol car still hadn't shown up in her rearview mirror when she slipped into traffic on I-90 and changed lanes until she was flanked by one semi to the right and another at her rear bumper for cover. *Please, God, be with me. Please.*

At the Elgin exit she white-knuckled the steering wheel. Held her breath. Then veered off at the last second and wound through the residential areas for twenty minutes, making sure no one had followed, before she headed for the far edge of the Metra commuter train parking lot and pulled in next to the battered Ford Focus she'd left there earlier, for the disappearance she'd planned for tomorrow.

Then, she waited.

Waited.

Waited.

Waited, her hands trembling and heart pounding, until the last train of the night left at 10:15, and no one was in sight. Each endless minute had ratcheted up her tension—but she couldn't risk the curiosity of anyone who might still be lingering in some unseen corner of the station. One misstep, and someone might remember her.

And then she would be as good as dead.

Finally, she pulled her hat low over her newly dyed auburn hair and quickly transferred her duffel bag and suitcases from the SUV into the trunk of the Focus.

After plugging in her GPS, she began her new route on quiet backcountry two-lane roads.

She had no doubt that her Blazer would be discovered in the morning. The shattered front and back windows would ensure a great deal of interest by the local police. The license plates would be easily traced to her latest identity.

But the Focus would buy her time.

Bought with cash from a sleazy little car lot in a bad part of town, she'd given the seller a false name she fabricated on the spot, stashed the car at the commuter train station. Then she'd taken the Metra downtown and used the city bus system for the final leg of the trip home.

Maybe her pursuers would expect she'd decided to lose herself among the eight million people of the Chicago area. With luck, that's exactly where they'd search, and eventually they would give up.

Now she just had to make it to the Greyhound bus station in Moline, on the Iowa-Illinois border, pay cash for a ticket to Deer Lodge, Montana, and catch the midnight departure.

And then finally she'd be free.

The Greyhound pulled off the freeway near Ogallala, Nebraska, and stopped at

a truck stop with a well-lit mom-and-pop
café. Next to it lay a parking lot overflowing with cars and trucks, and beyond that,
a Travelodge hotel with Welcome to the
Western States Regional Bowling Championship Contestants and No Vacancy lit
on its sign.

Through the café's large front windows
Emma could see a long lunch counter and
a half-dozen booths, already populated
by a crowd of trucker types hunched over
large coffee mugs and massive servings of
heart-attack-on-a-plate trucker specials.

The bus driver and the dozen other passengers piled out and made a beeline for
the café and restrooms. Emma wavered.
The darkness in the bus throughout the
night had been reassuring, the passengers
dozing and otherwise keeping to themselves. But bright lights and the intimacy
of the limited seating in the café could
provoke conversation and curiosity, something she'd worked hard to avoid.

The granola bars and cans of Coke in her

duffel would just have to do, along with the tiny restroom at the back of the bus.

She watched people come and go. A mom heading for the door to the café, gripping the hands of two toddlers bundled into heavy blue snowsuits. A gray-haired couple hanging on to each other for support as they came out and bent into the bitter wind, heading for the hotel with scarves wrapped around their faces.

A tall cowboy sauntered toward the gas station from his truck and horse trailer at the last gas pump, the brim of his Western hat pulled down low over his forehead.

One of the toddlers broke free as his mother opened the door, and made a beeline for the gas pumps just as a rattletrap of a pickup pulled off the highway into the lot, swung wide and started skidding sideways. The mother screamed and threw herself toward her child. Pedestrians swung around. The scene played out in slow motion.

The crushing weight of the truck sluiced

sideways, the side of its front wheel aimed straight for the child and coming too, too fast.

And suddenly the cowboy was there— diving for the child. Rolling in the snow, protecting him with his body. Even through the thick, well-insulated walls of the bus Emma heard an uproar of excited shouts as the young mother fell to her knees at the cowboy's side and opened her arms when he handed over her unharmed child.

The crowd grew around them, slapping the cowboy on the back, then some broke away and loudly confronted the driver of the pickup who staggered out of his truck and leaned against the front fender, pale and shaken and quite possibly drunk.

Emma leaned back, her own fear subsiding as she watched the mother wrap her arms around the cowboy in heartfelt thanks, then hold his hand for a moment. He touched the brim of his hat, then headed into the gas station, while she shepherded her children into the café.

A true hero, Emma thought, the one person among the many who had thought fast and acted in time. Why had she never run into someone like that when she'd needed him most?

She settled back in her seat and read a page of the book in her lap, then idly drew a circle in the frost that had already formed on her window. Rubbing out a bigger porthole, she drew in a sharp breath.

Impossible. She'd been so incredibly careful.

The chill from touching the icy glass rushed through her. Outside the door of the gas station, she could see the bus driver and the cowboy both holding foam to-go cups, listening to a tall man in a dark overcoat and gray dress slacks who was facing away from the bus. All three were hunched against the wind, their collars turned up.

From his rigid stance and forceful gestures it was apparent that the newcomer was agitated and demanding some sort of action. He pivoted and stood in front of the big plate glass window to stare at the people inside. Then he turned back to the bus driver and the cowboy and pointed toward the bus.

She stared at him, too horrified to move.

It was too far away to see his face, but he was tall, with the same kind of coat and gray slacks as the man she'd seen in her kitchen. It had to be a coincidence. How was it even *possible* that he could find her this far from Chicago? Unless…

The truth hit her like a punch to her stomach.

Had Todd planted a tracking device on her? Who would have ordered it—the good guys or bad? Either way, she was in trouble.

The man in the overcoat was already striding toward the bus, clearly planning to search inside.

There was no time to hunt for her luggage stowed in the belly of the bus, and even grabbing her duffel could spell danger if it held the tracking device. Grabbing only her purse, she crouched low and hurried to the exit, shoved the door open and bolted for the nearby row of semis along the edge of the parking lot, thankful that the bus had been parked with its exit door facing away from the café.

The semi tractors were idling to keep their diesel fuel warm and all were dark, so the drivers were either asleep inside with their doors locked or were over at the café. There was no time to search out someone in a sleeper cab and beg for shelter.

The wind sent sleet and cold down the collar of her coat as she hurried behind the trucks for cover, then hesitated. The hotel parking lot ahead was packed with cars and pickups, but few people left their vehicles open these days and only a fool left keys in an ignition. There'd be a slim chance of finding refuge there. The hotel itself was too far away—with a swath of open lawn between its front doors and the parking area. She would be spotted in an instant. *Please, God, help me find someone, someplace...*

Her frantic gaze landed on the rig at the farthest gas pump.

The pickup lights were off, but inside the back of the trailer, a horse whinnied. That cowboy would surely be back soon. Would he help her? Would he give her a ride? Or would he first demand answers that would take far too long?

Already, she could hear a male voice over by the bus. If the bus driver had told that guy about her being a passenger, she was in deep trouble.

Bending low, she crept to the horse trailer and nearly cried out in relief when she read its Montana plates. "Please, please be heading back home," she whispered to herself.

But the cab of the truck was still empty,

save for a big dog that surged toward the window from the shadows of the interior, its teeth bared.

The voice approached the other side of the horse trailer, apparently talking into a cell phone. So close that she could hear him breathing.

"I told you, I couldn't—not when I took out her old man. Too many witnesses. But when I get my hands on her, she ain't gonna die easy."

A wave of dizziness rushed through her and her heart threatened to batter its way out of her rib cage as she glanced wildly at her surroundings.

There was no other place to hide but here—unless she dared step out into the lights illuminating the truck stop parking area.

Her hands shaking, she tried the dressing room door at the front of the trailer. The handle turned easily and the door swung open, revealing a dark, cavernous space redolent of good leather and saddle soap and horse. *Thank you, God.*

Footsteps crunched in the snow, rounding the back of the trailer. A man cursed.

Her knees threatened to buckle as she slipped up into the dressing room compartment of the trailer and eased the door shut behind her. She took a quiet step back and tried to calm her rapid breathing. The jackhammer rate of her heartbeat echoed in her head—surely loud enough to be heard from outside.

In the dim light coming through the window in the door, she could make out a three-tier saddle rack. Bridles and other leather equipment hanging from hooks. A gun rack cradling a rifle, bolted high on the wall. On the floor were a tire rim and jack, a bag of Purina dog food and several bags of horse feed rich with the warm, sweet smell of molasses.

In the corner—thank you, Lord—was a big pile of winter horse blankets and a crumpled tarp.

She crawled under the blankets, thankful for the wind outside and praying that it masked the sounds of her movements, and wiggled as far back into the corner as she could. The smell of the horse blankets enveloped her…strong and pungent, but somehow the heavy weight of them felt comforting, secure.

A second later, the door hinges squealed as the compartment door was jerked open. The horse in the back whinnied, the noise reverberating through the trailer.

"Hey, what are you doing?" The new voice was deeper. Angry. "Get away from my trailer."

So this was the cowboy, then—the one who had saved the little boy.

"I already told you—I'm looking for a woman on the run. Cold-blooded killer."

"Well, as you can see, there's no one here." The dressing room door slammed. A key turned in the lock.

"I need to check the back of your trailer."

"Looks to me like you've got a few hundred other vehicles to check," the cowboy shot back, his voice laced with derision. "And you'd better get moving—I see at least three with headlights on that are gonna be leaving anytime."

"If she stowed away in your rig, you'd better be ready to watch your back, cowboy," the man growled, his voice so close to the trailer that Emma's heart skipped a beat. "I thought I saw something moving over here. I'm only trying to save you trouble."

Emma heard a pause, then a series of four drop-down feed doors along the side of the trailer squealed open and slammed shut, one by one.

"There. Are you satisfied?"

"No. She's got to be here somewhere." A set of footsteps crunched in the snow as the voice moved away.

Someone else—likely the cowboy—headed forward to the pickup. A truck door opened, then closed.

Emma crawled forward into a dim pool

of light coming through the foot-square window in the dressing room door and felt through her purse, then ran her fingertips along the seams. Underneath the zipper, she found it—a small, silver disk.

All of her careful efforts had been for nothing, because she'd had a tracking device planted on her all along.

Sickened, she waited until all was silent, and then she stood and surreptitiously slid the window open to throw the device over a bank of snow.

It might not be the only device they'd planted, but finding it was a start.

She would stay hidden in here, but she'd have the rifle in her hands and ready if the wrong person opened that door. And once she was far enough away from here, then she would slip away the first chance she had.

From outside she heard the familiar whoosh of the Greyhound as it rolled back toward the highway, paused, and lumbered away. Now the pickup engine roared to life. An overhead light in the dressing room compartment came on, and through a sliver of space in the back wall, she could see the lights were on in the interior of the horse compartment, as well.

A vibration shook through the trailer, and suddenly it was moving. Unfolding more of the blankets to create a warm nest, she tucked one around herself to guard against the chilled air.

It was cold in here. She had no idea where she was headed, or if she could trust the cowboy at the wheel. But if she'd stayed at the truck stop, she might have been found, and she had no illusions about where that would've led. At least now, she had at least a little more time to live.

She started to pray.

Jake Kincaid turned up the truck radio and scanned through the stations. Every frequency coming in loud and clear was focused on one thing: blizzard warnings—the last thing he wanted to deal with after three days on the road.

He flicked a glance in the side mirrors and saw only a wall of white billowing up behind his rig. Now and then another vehicle seemed to come out of nowhere, its headlights suddenly slicing through the heavy snowfall. Ahead, he could only see a couple dozen yards of snow-covered asphalt. Western Nebraska and the eastern edge of Colorado were being hit hard, but the worst of it had passed Denver. If he could just make it to the metropolitan area tonight, he'd be home free.

The Early Spring Color Breed Bonanza Sale was tomorrow, and the two horses in back were consigned. He'd been glad to have a load to help pay for the westward trip home, after hauling one of his champion roping geldings to its buyer in Illinois, but now the weather was giving him second thoughts.

The truck bucked through a drift and the trailer jerked and swayed. Between the narrow, high snowdrifts blowing across the highway like ribs on a skeleton, glare ice now stretched as far ahead as he could see, and the number of cars and trucks in the ditches on either side of the freeway was increasing with every mile. Sensing his tension, the golden lab on the seat next to him uncurled herself to sit upright.

He stroked her soft coat. "Looks like we'd better take this next rest stop, Maisie."

She whined and licked his cheek, thumping her tail against the upholstery.

He felt the vehicle lose traction, start to slide sideways, then the tires caught and straightened out. He slowed to a crawl, put on his flashers and eased off on the next ramp. The rest stop was already packed with semis and passenger cars, but at the end of the parking area he found one last double-long spot for a truck and trailer to pull in at an angle.

Maisie hopped out as soon as he opened the door and went to do her business in front of the bumper, then followed close at his heels when he went back to check on the horses. He'd just started to open the back gate of the trailer when the dog burst into a ferocious round of barking.

"Quiet," he shouted over the keening wind.

She barked even louder, her attention riveted on the dressing room door at the front of the trailer. If she wanted her dog food that bad, she must think she was really starving. "Okay, okay."

He reached down to ruffle her coat, then went to the backseat of the truck for a bottle of water and her two bowls. She growled when he reached for the door of the dressing room.

"What, did we pick up a mouse at the last barn?" He unlocked the door and reached inside to flip on the lights, which had gone out when he turned off the truck ignition, and scanned the insides, hoping it wasn't something larger than a mouse. The last thing he needed was to find that a barn cat had hitched a ride away from that last horse farm. Especially if it was a favorite of the trainer's children.

But it wasn't a barn cat staring at him from the far corner with wide hazel eyes, tousled auburn hair peeking from beneath a knitted hat, and pale skin turning blue with cold. It was a woman huddled in a pile of horse blankets, her teeth chattering and hands trembling.

And she had his rifle pointed straight at his chest.

TWO

Jake took a slow step back and raised his hands, palms up, as he assessed the situation.

The woman staring back at him appeared slender, late-twenties. Caucasian. Probably not more than a hundred-twenty pounds. Delicate bone structure and pretty in an upscale way. In other words, the last person he'd ever expect to find in his horse trailer in a pile of pungent horse blankets, in the middle of nowhere…during a blizzard.

She looked more like the type to be heading to Starbucks, rather than a woman who might be on the run from murder charges, but his ten years in law enforcement had taught him more than he'd ever wanted to know about how looks could be deceiving.

After his ex-wife proved it all over again, he'd become one very jaded man.

"Tell me you're not the woman that guy was looking for back in Ogallala," he said on a long sigh. "I really don't have time for this."

She raised the rifle, ready to sight her target—his chest—and gave him the answer he wanted. "I'm not."

A gust of wind-driven snow slammed against him and swirled into the dressing room of the trailer. "Let me rephrase that. Who are you, and why are you in my trailer?"

She was clearly cold, exhausted and desperate, her wild tangle of hair and the intensity in her eyes suggesting that she just might pull the trigger if he pushed her too far.

She visibly shivered, and the barrel of his rifle wobbled. "I...I hid in here when you stopped last."

"In *Sterling?*" Not likely. He'd padlocked the dressing room door back in Ogallala. She couldn't have gained access after that.

Apparently she realized her error. "I...I must've fallen asleep. I don't remember Sterling."

"Why don't you come on out of there and we can talk about it."

She shook her head.

"You look cold and my dog and I are standing out in a blizzard. My pickup is warmer." When she didn't respond, he shrugged. "I'll tell you what. If you want to thaw, come to my truck. If not, this door is open and you can skedaddle. Far as I'm concerned, this just isn't worth dying over."

"Wh-where are we?"

"Nowhere close to where I need to be. This here is a freeway rest stop, so there are lots of other vehicles for you to choose from. Tell someone a story about how your car is in a ditch somewhere. If you don't go pointing that rifle at them, they might think you're a nice girl and offer you a ride."

She huddled farther back into the pile of horse blankets, her eyes huge in her pale face. She looked scared to death. "I—I can't."

"Maisie and I are going to go get warm." He touched the brim of his hat. "You're welcome to join me. If you don't, I'll just have to trust that you won't haul off my saddles or my rifle when you leave."

He opened the door of the truck and let Maisie into the front seat, then slid behind the wheel and glanced at the clock. Five minutes. Ten. The woman still hadn't shown up. "What do you think, old girl? Should we see if she's still back there?"

The dog gave him a reproving look.

A moment later, he heard a soft knock on the passenger side. "Maisie, back."

The dog jumped into the backseat as the front door squealed open and the woman climbed in, the rifle still in her hands and a big leather purse slung on her shoulder. Her lips were blue and her teeth were chattering so loudly that he could hear them across the seat.

He nudged the heater up a notch. "Glad you could make it."

She huddled into the corner, as far from him as she could get.

He tapped the insulated coffee mug in the center divider. "It's cold now, but you could pretend."

"Y-you said you stopped in Sterling. Are you going to Montana?"

"Eventually."

She looked up at him in alarm. *"Eventually?"*

"Why, are you heading for someplace special?"

She didn't answer. Pulling off her thin leather gloves, she blew on her hands and rubbed them together.

"Maybe we could start with a name. That oughta be easy. I'm Jake Kincaid. And you are…"

"Emma," she whispered after a long silence. "Emma…White."

If that was her name, he'd eat his Stetson, but at least it was a start. "Okay, Emma White. How come you stowed away in my trailer? All you had to do was ask for a ride."

Her answering laugh was bitter. "And you would have picked up some stranger, just like that, and risk being robbed. Or worse."

Raising an eyebrow, he dropped his gaze to the rifle in her hands. "Looks like that might be happening anyway."

She stared at the weapon as if it had turned into a rattler, then she leaned it against her door. "No."

"That man in Ogallala said he was looking for a woman wanted for murder. Despite your first answer, I'm guessing he was hunting for you. Am I wrong?"

After a long silence, she finally nodded. "If that was who I think it was, he told you a flat-out lie. If he caught me, I'd be the one who was dead."

"He said the authorities were after you too, lady."

She shivered. "If you think they're all good people, you're naive." She stared pensively through the windshield at the swirling snow, as if debating about what to say. "That was...um...my ex-boyfriend."

"Now, why would you be chasing off in weather like this, if you weren't on the run from some serious charges? Seems to me you'd want to pick a nicer day. And maybe it would have been easier to just tell him to get lost."

She flicked a quick, pained glance at him, not quite meeting his eyes, then she looked away. "I know you can't relate. But tell me what *you'd* do, if you were a woman and an abusive man was threatening to tear you apart. Randy is a big guy, and when he starts drinking, he gets violent. Once, he even kicked in the door of my apartment. I always tried to stay out of his way. But it never worked in the past, and this time he came after me with a gun."

Jake cocked an eyebrow. "How did you get mixed up with someone like that?"

She shuddered. "It was the biggest mistake of my life. Believe me."

"Why didn't you leave a long time ago?" He'd been involved in far too many domestic calls when he'd worked as a deputy in western Wyoming. He knew the answer already—leaving could be as dangerous as sticking around. But something just didn't ring true in this woman's voice.

"I tried once. He swore he'd track me down and kill me if I tried to leave town." She visibly shuddered. "And this time he was so out of control that I knew he'd do it if I stayed. I *had* to run."

"Did he hurt you?"

"Not yet. I…hitchhiked as far as that truck stop, and when I saw he'd caught up with me, I knew my only choice was to run, or die. So I hid in your trailer."

Jake had no doubt that she was frightened, but not for the reasons she gave. He could see she was lying in the way she fidgeted and avoided meeting his eyes. Mentally reviewing what she'd just said, he rested a wrist on the top of the steering wheel and studied the falling snow.

"Sooo…if I make a phone call and check out your story, my sources will back you up?"

"I don't know." She slumped against the seat, her voice weary.

"What about previous assault charges against him? Would I find some of those?"

Her gaze darted to his, then skated away again. "I never dared. It's a small town, and Randy's brother is a cop. Even if I'd called 9-1-1 and had him arrested, Randy would've been back on my doorstep in no time, and I don't even want to know what would've happened then."

"Restraining orders?"

"Like I said, I was afraid to take the first step. With him, a court order would be like waving a red cape in front of a bull." She sighed heavily. "For all I know, Randy and his brother have trumped up charges against me, just to make sure that someone, somewhere, will arrest me and send me back home."

If her words hadn't sounded so rehearsed, he might have believed her. Than again, maybe it was a situation she'd been mulling over for a long time. "So you're telling me that you don't want me calling the cops."

"Look, I know you don't know me. I'm really sorry about pointing a gun at you, but I'm honestly a nice person, and all I'm asking is that you not do that. If you can just give me a ride to the next town, I can start making my way to Montana."

"What town?"

"Deer Lodge."

"You have relatives there?"

She hesitated, then shook her head.

"You aren't sure, or you just don't know them?" He thought a moment. "Or maybe you have someone there on a semipermanent basis?"

"What?"

"Temporary housing at the Montana State Prison?"

"No! I…I'm just going to start over, that's all. And that's all you need to know about me."

"So if I drop you off at the next town, what then? Do you have money for a bus ticket, or are you going to stow away in the next horse trailer you see?"

She drew herself up. "I'll be fine."

"Right. Do you have any money? Credit or debit cards?"

Again, the flicker in her gaze. "I'm set. And I'm not your responsibility, so don't worry about it."

And that was the kicker in this whole, strange and unexpected deal. *Responsibility.*

He'd felt the weight of the world on his

shoulders when he'd worked in law enforcement...and one case in particular still haunted him. He and the rest of the department had put in sixteen-hour days, trying to solve a serial rapist case that had terrified women throughout the county. In the meantime, four more women were attacked...including his sister's best friend.

Could he blithely ignore the possibility that this woman was in real danger? The thought cut through him like a switchblade between the ribs.

He sighed heavily. When he arose this morning at four-thirty, he'd had no idea just how complicated his life was going to become. "You can't just go hitchhiking into some remote part of the country. I don't believe you do have the money for another bus ticket, and whoever he really is, there's no denying that someone is trying to hunt you down. So lady, give me your driver's license. If you check out okay, I've got a proposition for you."

* * *

Emma's heartbeat faltered as she stared back at him.

She'd always been a terrible liar and hated needing to skate around the truth, even though she'd been living a lie throughout most of her life in WITSEC. Jake had probably seen through every one of the whoppers she'd just told.

An abusive *ex-boyfriend?* Named *Randy?*

All of it was straight out of a novel she'd just read, and now she was going to be caught up in a web of those lies, trying to keep things straight, unless she managed to part company with this guy...and soon.

If he had a proposition, she could only imagine that it spelled trouble. Still, to flee instead of calmly letting him check her license would set off alarm bells in his mind and lead to more trouble than she was already in. Please, God, help me out, here.

"License?" Jake repeated. "Or is it conveniently missing?"

"O-of course not." She bent over her purse and pawed through the contents, delaying the inevitable.

No one upstairs ever seemed to listen to her prayers, but during the twenty-four hours since she'd fled her home, Emma had found herself saying a lot of them, and now she mentally recited yet another as she pulled out her wallet and handed over her freshly minted driver's license. "I'm sure everything is in order."

She hoped. During her ten years in the WITSEC program she'd had plenty of new identities come and go, but this was the first time she'd created one on her own.

She'd paid a thousand dollars to a guy with the unlikely name of Lance Mendez for her new identification, but whether or not good customer service and guarantees were part of the business model used by furtive men on street corners wasn't hard to guess.

"Lance" had been recommended by a man she'd approached outside a seedy bar on the lower south side of Chicago, the day after her father's murder. She'd never been so terrified in her life, driving into that unfamiliar neighborhood.

But she'd never been so desperate, either, and knowing that her dad's killer would have her in his sights next, her choice had been simple. Die, or disappear.

Now, she tried to look bored as the cowboy studied her, then shot another glance at her driver's license. "Can you take off that hat?"

She'd worn the cheap knitted hat with a floppy brim in public since cutting her long blond hair short and dying it auburn several days ago, afraid her father's killer might be stalking her. She'd wanted to hide the new color until she could reveal a totally different persona when she surfaced a thousand miles away.

She took a quick, furtive glance out the truck windows, then slowly dragged it off and ran her fingers through her hair to fluff the flattened curls. She jerked it back on a moment later.

"Traveling kinda light, aren't you, ma'am?"

"I didn't exactly have time to pack well," she murmured, forcing herself to meet his eyes.

No wonder Jake was suspicious. She smelled like a dirty horse blanket and hadn't washed her face in a good twenty-four hours. Her suitcase was still on that bus, headed to who knows where. She'd fled Chicago without a brush, makeup or even the most basic toiletries in her purse.

Jake probably thought she appeared homeless, deranged and desperate; capable of any charges that had been trumped up to reel her back to Chicago. The murder of Todd Hlavicek, for instance, unless he was still lying on her kitchen floor.

Jake compared her against her license photo one more time, then grabbed a cell phone from the dashboard of the truck, scrolled through his contacts list and hit

Send. "Megan. This is Jake. Right, it's been a while." He sighed. "No, not anytime soon. Probably never. Hey, I need a favor. Can you run a driver's license for me?"

Emma jerked her hat back on and forced a smile, though an icy hand clamped around her stomach as Jake read off her license number and description. Lance had needed a photo of her for the driver's license, so she'd gone to a drugstore passport photo booth right after dying her hair and cutting it short. Did the license look realistic enough? Would the number actually work, or was her false identity going to shatter, here and now?

The woman Jake called apparently put him on hold.

He moved the cell phone away from his face. "I've got Megan Peters on the line. She's the new Pine County sheriff up in Montana, and an old friend of mine. Is she gonna find out things about you that you don't want me to know?"

"Only if there are errors in the system." Emma feigned a disinterested shrug, even though her insides were shaking.

The minutes dragged like hours. Weeks.

Then Jake sat up a little straighter and carried on a cursory conversation before ending the call and tossing his phone back onto the dash. A corner of his mouth tipped up in a faint smile. "Megan did a little research. The internet is just one amazing thing, isn't it?

His folksy demeanor didn't fool her for a minute. "And?"

"She checked the NCIS, NCIC and CODIS, and you weren't listed in any of them."

"What does all of *that* mean?"

"That you've got a ride to Montana, if you want it. Apparently—at this point— you're not a fugitive, missing person, or someone of interest in the criminal databases. I fact, your name is *unusually* clean. No charges, ever. No convictions, no warrants, no moving violations. Not even a traffic ticket. No record of property ownership, for that matter. It's as if you just dropped out of the sky."

Throwing up her hands and shouting "Thank you, Lance!" probably wouldn't be a good thing right now. She smiled. "I told you so."

His lips thinned. "There's still something that isn't quite right about this, but I don't want to leave a lone woman to fend for herself at this rest stop, so I can either drop you off at the next town, or drop you off when I go through Denver. Or, you can ride with me until I get back to Montana, and I can leave you off in Deer Lodge. Your choice."

"Deer Lodge? *Really?* You're heading that way?"

"It's not my destination, but I can take a detour."

Hope surged through her, then fizzled away. She didn't even want to think about what he might expect in return. "I…I'd better get out at the next place there could be a bus stop."

"If you're short on cash, I can loan you hotel money. With the horse sale and all, it'll take me a couple days to get up to Deer Lodge."

She bit her lower lip. Did she dare trust him? Her heart said yes, but every cautious bone in her body was saying *no, no, no*. Yet what other option did she have? Her pursuers were probably watching the bus lines and airports. If she tried to catch a different ride, the vehicle she approached could be driven by the very people she was trying to avoid.

Given the money behind the Rodriguez drug cartel, there could be any number of people after her, now that the location of the house she and her family had shared had been discovered. And they could be men—or women—whom she might not be able to identify until it was too late.

"Believe me when I say that you're safe with me. I have no designs on you at all.

None," he added, his mouth kicking up into a wry grin. "You aren't my type."

No surprise, there…but what should have felt like an insult just gave her a sense of relief.

He was tall and powerfully built, with a strong jaw and dimples that flashed when he grinned. Adding in the long dark lashes shading his melted chocolate eyes, he looked like he could be in magazine ads for Levi's jeans or big, tough pickup trucks. His taste probably ran to curvaceous, surgically enhanced blondes with Botox lips and empty smiles.

If such a vacuous creature existed in the wilds of Montana, anyway.

"Then what's in this for you?"

He laughed at that. "Oh, I still think you're in trouble. This'll just give me a few days to figure it all out."

THREE

After hours of heavy snow and high winds buffeting the side of his rig, the wind finally slowed and Jake heard the approaching roar of a snowplow swinging up through the rest stop.

Wrapped in blankets and asleep for the past two hours, Emma didn't even stir when the mammoth vehicle thundered by, its blade scraping and clattering and kicking up sparks against the asphalt. He studied the violet circles of exhaustion under her eyes and the lines of tension between her delicate eyebrows, and felt a pang of sympathy. She spelled trouble, no two ways around it.

But even without makeup and her short hair in disarray, she was still a pretty little thing, with those big hazel eyes and the dark crescents of her lashes resting on her delicate cheeks. She was far too fragile to be out here in the middle of nowhere, alone and defenseless. What if she'd stumbled into the wrong stranger's vehicle and had ended up a bloodied statistic in some roadside ditch?

He had no business getting involved.

Not after the last phone call he'd received from Uncle Oliver, about more trouble brewing of his own.

But there was no way he could let her fend for herself, either, and Megan had promised to let him know if Emma turned up on any new warrants coming through. He'd keep a tight hold on his wallet and a watchful eye on Emma, and in just a couple of days he'd drop her off in Deer Lodge. End of story.

He'd turned on the truck every once in a while to ward off the bitter cold outside. Now, he took Maisie for a quick trip outside, and then he ushered her into the backseat, slid behind the wheel and headed back onto the freeway.

Patches of ice gleamed bare and dangerous between stretches of snow-packed asphalt. Intermittent gusts of snow obliterated the road ahead, threatening to fill in the swath of the snowplow, but at least he was on his way.

He glanced at the clock on the dash and sighed heavily. "Ma'am? You'd better put on your seat belt."

The blankets stirred. He angled a look in Emma's direction and saw her blink, then sit up in startled confusion. There was no mistaking that flash of fear in her eyes or the way she visibly reined in her emotions before she settled back against the seat and fastened her seat belt.

"Nice nap?" he drawled.

"Wh-where are we?"

"Heading for Denver, but it's going to be a long haul in this weather."

She pulled the blanket tighter around her shoulders. "How long will it take?"

"The sales arena is west of Denver, and my GPS says it's four hours away. But that's on a *good* day. Tonight? It could easily be double that. Maybe more."

Her brow furrowed. "Will you get there in time for…for whatever?"

"The sale starts at nine in the morning. Cataloged horses have to be checked onto the grounds by 7:00 a.m. sharp."

"If you're late?"

"The sale barn rules say they'll put us at the end of the sales lineup for the day. Which is just about the time most of the buyers have loaded up and started home."

Her forehead furrowed. "That would be bad."

He shrugged. "My guess is that there'll be a lot of trailers pulling in late, and they'll do the best to keep everyone happy. But if not, there's nothing I can do about it."

She eyed him thoughtfully. "You sound pretty philosophical. Some guys would be awfully upset."

"No point."

Her short laugh sounded bitter. "There doesn't have to be one."

He'd doubted her earlier story about an avenging ex-boyfriend and his cop buddy. Now, he wasn't so sure. "When I started for Denver this morning I left in plenty of time, and there wasn't anything in the forecast about snow."

"Tell me about it," she muttered, surreptitiously glancing at the side mirror outside her window.

"The owner of the horses ought to know that as well as I do. No sense ending up in a ditch trying to hurry." The snow swirled up into a white wall ahead and he eased up on the accelerator until the visibility improved. "If you're feeling edgy, you can probably relax. Even if someone passes us, they won't be able to see you. Not at night."

"I'll just feel a lot better when there are a few hundred miles more between me and Ogallala." She shifted uneasily. "Maybe that guy wrote down your license plate number. People can track down way too much information these days."

"Oh?"

"Go online with a credit card, and you can find out *everything* about someone." She twisted in her seat to look at him. "You seem like a nice guy. I never should've gotten you mixed up in my problems."

He lifted a shoulder. "I'm not too concerned."

"But—"

"If you turn out to be a felon, I'll deal with it."

"I'm not."

For the first time in three years, he felt an old, familiar surge of adrenaline, and realized he'd missed the excitement and danger of his old career. "Then if some bad guys are after you, I guess I can handle that, too. No worries."

"For you, maybe," she retorted drily. "But thanks."

Despite a few hours of sleep at the freeway rest area, Emma still felt bone tired. But with the truck bucking and swaying through growing snowdrifts and the terrifying shimmy when she felt the wheels lose traction across an icy patch, her attention stayed riveted on the road ahead.

By the time they reached the grounds of the horse show arena at nearly five in the morning, the snow had stopped and the highways were clear. Jake pulled to a stop in front of the main entrance of vast building with *Horses* painted above the doors. A single outdoor security light blazed above the sign, though the rest of the parking area was pitch-dark.

He slumped against the seat and angled a look at her. "I've got stalls here, reserved under the horses' lot numbers. Once I find the stalls I need to get them bedded down and the horses settled, then I'll park the trailer and drop you off at a motel."

The last hours of battling bad roads and poor visibility had consumed her thoughts, but now she felt a renewed frisson of unease slip through her. "There's one close by?"

"A few miles."

"What about you?"

He wearily rolled his head against the neck rest to look at her. "I need to be here in a couple hours anyway. I'll just doze in the truck and set my cell phone alarm."

"I might as well stay here, too." She shifted uncomfortably. "It's not worth getting a room for such a short time."

"Go ahead—there's nothing for you to do here, and maybe you can sleep till noon or so. I'll pay for two nights so you won't have to check out." A corner of his mouth kicked up into a tired grin. "If the motel I'm thinking about has a room available, you'll find a dollar store a few doors down."

His thoughtfulness surprised her. Most of those stores carried basic clothing and toiletries, and just the thought of a long, hot shower and clean clothes was pure bliss. "Let me help you here. Can I carry anything?"

"I'll bring in the horses and feed. But if you want to grab a couple of water buckets out of the trailer, I'd appreciate it. I'm sure there must be spigots inside the building."

Pulling her hat down over her ears, she zipped up her jacket and stepped out into the cold. After finding the buckets in the dressing room of the trailer, she followed Jake, Maisie and the two horses into the building.

It was wonderfully warm inside, pungent with the rich scents of hay and horse and leather. Dim lights glowed from up in the rafters. Horses already in the stalls stirred, rustling their bedding and nickering as Jake led the mares down a long aisle, the metallic four-beat clip-clop of their shoes echoing in the cavernous space.

"This place is huge," she whispered as she watched him snug up each mare's blanket surcingles and put her in the appropriate stall.

"There are indoor and outdoor arenas on the grounds, one of the biggest sales barns in the country, and five hundred stalls here in the horse barn, I think."

The sharp angles and planes of his jaw, darkened by five o'clock shadow, gave him the air of a rugged, handsome hero on the Western reruns she often watched late at night, and there'd always been something about a confident, skilled and easygoing man that had appealed to her...maybe because nothing in her life had ever been stable.

Watching Jake stirred feelings that had no place in her life right now, and she struggled for a moment, trying to recall the conversation. "So this is a horse palace."

The corners of his eyes crinkled. "Not quite. You oughta see some of the horse operations in Texas and Oklahoma."

"And where you come from?"

He laughed at that. "Where I come from, things are just a tad more rustic."

"But beautiful, I'm sure."

He gave her an odd look. "You're sure you want to go someplace where you don't know a soul?"

"I may know...someone. But it's been many years, now. I'm not even sure I can find her." *Or if I dare.* Bringing trouble to her sister's door after all this time was the last thing she wanted to do. "So, where do I find water for these buckets?"

He nodded toward the end of the aisle. "Go down there, take a left. I think there are faucets just around the corner. I'll go back outside and get the grain, hay and ground feeders."

Maisie followed at Jake's heels as he

strode back toward the entrance. Emma walked down the aisle, listening to the sounds of his fading footsteps as she passed another dozen horses in stalls, six on each side of the aisle. Most were dozing, heads low and a hind hoof cocked, or laying down. A couple of them moved up against the vertical bars at the front of their stalls and eyed her expectantly, as if hoping for early breakfast.

Beyond those horses was a long stretch of empty stalls, the stall doors open, the interiors shadowed and dark as the mouth of a cave. She felt a prickle of unease crawl across the back of her neck as she passed each one.

The barn had seemed warm and welcoming when she'd first arrived, alive with the peaceful presence of the horses. Back here, anything—or anyone—could be lying in wait for her.

But of course, that was ridiculous.

No one from Chicago could've predicted that she would be here. The man she'd seen back in Ogallala would've had to battle the same tough winter conditions if he'd tried to follow, and with such poor visibility he would've had to second-guess every exit, wondering if Jake might've turned off and headed for parts unknown.

Until she and Jake reached the Denver metro area, she'd never even noticed any headlights in the rearview mirror, other than those of a few semis that had crawled slowly past. And she certainly hadn't heard anyone enter the building since they'd arrived here.

Taking a deep breath, she reached the end of the aisle and turned the corner. Sure enough, there was the water spigot a few yards ahead for filling buckets. "Just a few minutes more, and I'll be in some nice comfy motel," she muttered under her breath. "Door locked, nice and safe."

Warm, stale breath fanned across the back of her neck. *Or did it?*

A hand clamped down on her shoulder, the fingers digging painfully into the

hollow above her collarbone. The cloying order of cheap aftershave filled her
nostrils.

"Stop right there."

She froze as panic raced through her.

"I wouldn't make a sound, if I were you.
Now drop those buckets, nice and easy,
and start walking. We're going to make
a phone call and take care of you, believe
me."

Her heart lurched. All of the lights were
off in this section of the barn. The shad-
owy aisle ahead faded into complete darkness. It was the last direction she dared
go—yet her attacker behind her stood between her and possible safety with Jake.

Jake.

What if he was…what if he was already
dead?

She forced herself to take a step. Then
another, her thoughts racing, her knees
weak with fear. Two things were clear.
Cooperation would leave her dead. With

an escape attempt, it was just a strong possibility.

"*Please*—just let me go."

The grip on her shoulder tightened as the man behind her forced her to walk faster. "Shut up."

His voice grated across her skin. She edged a hand into her jacket pocket, praying that her car keys were still there. Fought back the shivers racing through her as she judged her surroundings. "You've got the wrong person. Honest. I—"

"You've caused enough trouble already," the man snarled, giving her shoulder a sharp jerk.

She surreptitiously unzipped her jacket a millimeter at a time, offered a fast, silent prayer, then she slashed at his fingers with the jagged edge of her car key and let her knees buckle.

"Hey!" He clawed at her loosened jacket, his grasp broken. She spun around. Rammed her elbow into his side. He swore, flailing his arms as he stumbled sideways and fell, but he was at her heels in a split second, grabbing for her collar.

She struggled. Slipped free of the jacket. Then she raced back toward the way they'd come, screaming Jake's name, skidding on the smooth cement as she rounded the corner, her heart thundering and her lungs raw.

Somewhere ahead, she heard Maisie break into furious barking, the sounds coming closer. The dog burst into view around the corner and Emma dared a glance back.

In the next heartbeat she slammed into a solid wall of muscle. Powerful arms surrounded her. Maisie anxiously danced at her feet, whining and jumping up against her.

Emma screamed, fought to escape.

"Emma." Her captor loosened his grasp. "Emma, it's me. *Listen* to me."

It was Jake. Relief flooded through her, followed by another wave of fear. She threw another wild glance over her shoulder and saw only an empty aisle behind her. "Th-there's a man. He's back there. He—he grabbed me."

Jake held her at arm's length and studied her face for a second, then looked over her shoulder. "Quiet."

They both stood still, listening. All she could hear was the uneasy rustlings of the horses she'd just passed.

"He was back there," she said urgently. "He *was*. He tried to make me go with him."

"I believe you." Jake frowned. "Where's your jacket? You must be cold."

"He was grabbing for me. It—it fell off back there."

Jake reached for a cell phone clipped to his belt. "I'll call the cops."

That wasn't a good idea, and now another kind of fear sped through her.

Too many questions, a deputy's request to see her ID, and in an instant, her chance to slip into anonymity somewhere in Montana would go up in smoke. Being in police custody back in Chicago wouldn't guarantee her safety. If the powerful Rodriguez family learned she was there, money could exchange hands and she'd be a defenseless, easy target.

Alarmed, she shook her head. "No—really. Let's just leave. The sound of patrol cars coming would make that guy disappear into the night anyway. I'm not injured. There's no proof of anything."

"I'm taking you out to the truck. Stay in there with Maisie and lock the doors while I take a look around. Do you have a cell phone?"

This option was even worse.

"Don't go back there. It's not worth the risk. Please—let's just go."

"Don't worry about it. Now, do you have a cell phone?" His voice was gentle, but laced with steel, and she knew there'd be no point in arguing.

She nodded once, hoping the prepaid, anonymous cell phone she'd bought at a drugstore still held a charge.

"Come on." He took her hand and headed for the front door. At an electrical panel just inside the entrance, he studied the switches, then flooded the entire interior of the building in blazing lights. Horses whinnied. One of them kicked the side of its stall.

If her attacker had decided to flee the bright light in the building at this moment, any sound had been lost in the racket.

Jake settled her in the truck, with Maisie in the backseat, then he reached across her lap to put a key in the ignition and start the engine. "Stay warm. If you see anything, call 9-1-1, then start honking and keep at it. Nonstop. Don't hesitate, understand?"

"Please, you're not armed—what if something happens?"

A wry smile briefly touched his lips as he retrieved a gun from the glove box. "Then your friend will soon have second thoughts."

She blinked. "But he could be hiding in the building, and he could get you before you even knew where he was. At least take your dog with you."

"I want her here." Jake rested a hand on her arm. "Now look at me."

His voice was low, warm, compelling. She slowly lifted her gaze to meet his.

"I was a deputy for ten years. I'm not a careless man. But I've found it's sometimes better to seek out a rattler instead of leaving it be. Understand?"

She nodded, too numb to answer.

"But don't go calling 9-1-1 just because I'm not back right away. If I don't show up in thirty minutes, drive to the nearest well-lit gas station and make your call then. Not before."

He hit the lock button on the inside of her door and slammed it shut. And then he disappeared into the night.

FOUR

She'd wrapped herself in the blanket as soon as she got into Jake's pickup, but she couldn't stop shivering as the minutes ticked by.

Five.

Ten.

Fifteen.

Each interminable minute seemed like an hour, with her guilt and fear over Jake's safety holding her heart in an icy grip. *God, please watch over him. He seems like a nice guy. He doesn't deserve to get hurt. Not over this. Not because of me.*

She gripped her cell phone and peered

out into the darkness. She already knew that her attacker was far stronger than she was. For all she knew, he was armed and dangerous, and if cornered might not hesitate to shoot. Getting out of the truck and going after Jake herself fell into the too-stupid-to-live category.

But even if Jake had made it clear that she shouldn't call 9-1-1 for at least thirty minutes, who knew it would seem like this long? He could be lying on the cold cement floor in that barn, bludgeoned from behind or shot. No matter what happened to her if the police became involved in this, she couldn't let another moment pass.

She started pressing the buttons. 9…1…

"Emma! It's me."

Startled, she look up and quickly scanned the darkness.

"Over here." Jake stepped out of the gloom at the corner of the building. "And I've got someone with me."

Wary now, she twisted in the seat and

tried to make out the features of the person limping beside him. The two of them made their way slowly to the side of the truck.

She hesitated, her finger poised over the window button on the inner door.

"I found your 'attacker,'" Jake said quietly. "But Tom is a little worse for wear. And if you don't want the police involved, I think you'd better talk to him."

She blinked. Then lowered the window halfway.

The man next to Jake was a good five inches shorter and fifty pounds heavier, wearing a well-worn denim jacket and a heavy growth of salt-and-pepper beard. He glared at her as he rubbed his left shoulder with a bloodied hand.

"This—this is the man who grabbed me?" She resisted the urge to close the window and retreat to the far corner of the front seat.

"You were trespassing," Tom snarled.

Jake rested a hand on his uninjured

shoulder. "Apparently they've had considerable problems with theft from the barns here. So now they keep at least one barn hand on duty twenty-four hours a day."

"He threatened me!"

"I wasn't gonna let some thief get away, missy. I could lose my job."

"I wasn't stealing anything."

"So you say. I needed to hang on to you and call for help. Only you slashed my fingers and made me fall, and if this ripped up my rotator cuff again, I'm going to call the police and press charges against you for assault."

"Y-you *work* here?"

"That's what your friend just said."

Embarrassment started crawling through her. "Oh."

"And you were sneaking around in the dark."

"I was just getting some water. That's all." She bit her lower lip, wondering if she really believed him. But Jake apparently did, so she finally nodded. "I'm sorry that you got hurt."

"Humph." He scowled at her.

"No, really. I am. Is there anything I can do?"

"No. You'll be gone soon enough." Muttering under his breath, the older man hobbled back to the barn.

When he disappeared inside, she sank against her seat and watched Jake climb behind the steering wheel of the truck. "Well, that was embarrassing. Now you're going to think I've been crying wolf all this time."

"Could've been worse. He took a pretty hard fall, apparently." He handed over her jacket. "I found this on the floor by the water spigot."

"I was already jumpy, but then he came out of nowhere and clamped a hand on my shoulder. He scared me half to death." She tried for a rueful smile. "He was like my worst nightmare. But now you probably don't believe a word I've said."

"About being threatened?" He glanced over at her as he buckled his seat belt. "Remember, I did meet your old boyfriend back in Ogallala."

"About that...." She fell silent and looked away, uncomfortable with the lie she'd told. Unsure of what she could dare share with Jake now.

He turned on the ignition, then shifted the truck into drive and headed toward the field marked Trailer Parking that they'd passed when they'd first pulled into the grounds. "I don't think you need to worry. Even if he did see my license plate back in Ogallala or at that truck stop and traced it, he'd have no idea that I was heading to this sale. And I don't think we were followed."

"I hope not."

"We were both checking the rearview mirrors, and I sure didn't see anything suspicious. Of course, once we hit the freeways in Denver, it's anyone's guess. One set of headlights in the dark looks pretty much like the others from a distance, and I wouldn't even know what kind of vehicle to be watching for."

"Me neither," Emma said, trying to not sound as edgy as she felt. "But think about it. A guy who just *happened* to be in the barn at the moment we arrived? Ready to pounce on a lone woman who suddenly showed up in the middle of the night? Maybe that guy wasn't really a barn worker at all. Maybe he just came up with that cover when you confronted him."

"He looked nothing like the man back in Ogallala. And he also has a Colorado driver's license."

"You *checked?*"

Jake shrugged, a corner of his mouth lifting briefly. "A flashback to my cop days, I guess."

But there could easily be others who had been sent after her—not just the man in Ogallala. And how could she explain that? It would hardly fit with the story about her troublesome ex-boyfriend.

Jake drove into a parking spot. She

twisted in her seat and watched him un-hitch the trailer, breathing a sigh of relief when he finally got behind the wheel again and turned toward the highway. "Maybe you should get a room at the motel, too. I don't think it's safe out here."

He pulled to a stop at the stoplight, flipped on the turn signal and pulled out onto the two-lane asphalt road lead-ing back into town. "I guess I'd still just as soon hang around and make sure the horses are safe, and be sure I get them checked in on time."

"Then maybe I should stay out here with you. The motel probably doesn't even accept guests at this hour."

He angled a grin at her, the dimple bracketing his cheek deepening. "I never thought I'd hear a woman turn down luxury accommodations. I checked out the address and phone number on my iPhone, and made your reservation over an hour ago. They said they've got some basic supplies at the front desk, like toothbrushes and such. You're all set."

"Oh."

"And don't worry about the bill. I reserved it with my credit card. You can pay me back sometime when you have a job."

"Thanks. I'll pay back every penny. I promise."

Ahead, a cluster of businesses appeared, and beyond them, a pink, bird-shaped neon sign spelling out most of the letters for The Flam ngo Motel. Good Rates flashed in front of a twelve-unit strip motel. Cars were nosed up to the doors of four of the units closest to the office at one end.

Jake pulled to a stop in front of the office, where the blue, flickering light of a television danced against the curtains. He disappeared inside for a few minutes, then came out and tossed her a room key and a small plastic case holding a little tube of toothpaste and a new toothbrush.

"You've got the end unit, so it should

be more quiet," he said as he drove to the opposite end of the parking lot. "The old guy behind the desk says there's a diner a block farther down this street. I'll come back to check on you in the morning."

"You're really going to stay at the sales arena?" A wistful note crept into her voice and she forced herself to stand a little straighter. She'd be just fine, here. There were plenty of people around.

"I'll go back out there after I fill up my truck. The clerk said there's a twenty-four hour truck stop maybe five miles ahead." He handed her a business card. "This has my cell number on it, and don't hesitate to use it. If you need to call the motel office, just dial zero on the room phone."

Until this moment, she'd half expected him to take off tonight and never show up again, leaving her behind. A day ago, she wouldn't have cared, but now she realized just how blessed she'd been to run into someone like him. "I'll be fine."

He touched the brim of his hat and

waited until she unlocked the motel room door and turned on the interior lights, then he climbed back in his truck. "Sleep tight."

"Thanks, Jake." She stepped inside the small room, locked and chained the door, and leaned against it.

The room spelled of disinfectant, the carpet was threadbare, the furnishings cheap and minimal. But at least it looked clean. She should feel *relieved* to be here, off the road and in a safe place after a long and difficult night. That she hadn't needed to dip into her limited supply of cash was even better.

So why was a sense of dread now coiling her stomach into a knot?

Emma roamed the room, checking the windows and locks, then finally brushed her teeth and cleaned up as best she could at the cramped sink in the bathroom.

She felt dirty. Her clothes still reeked from the hours she'd spent wrapped in those horse blankets in the trailer. But with no luggage and no clean clothes, the thought of showering and putting the same clothes back on was as bad as just skipping the process until morning, when she could hike to that dollar store and pick up some cheap, basic clothing.

She pulled off her jeans and folded them over the back of a small wooden chair in the corner, then slipped into bed and stared at the ceiling, listening to the rattle of the fan in the wall heating unit.

But as exhausted as she felt, sleep wouldn't come.

Images of Todd flooded back through her thoughts; his congenial face twisted in agony. Had he betrayed her family?

It certainly made sense.

He was the only one who had known the address. Her father had been gunned down in cold blood. And a week later, she'd found two intruders in her house, standing over Todd's body.

Whether or not Todd had been the only

target that night, if she'd arrived sooner or had made a slower escape, she might already be dead, too.

The heater coughed and sputtered to a halt and silence descended. *Almost.*

Except for the soft and furtive footsteps just outside her door.

Jake finished filling up the truck, pulled the receipt from the gas pump and slid it into his wallet with his credit card. At four in the morning there was no one else here except for a lone attendant inside the convenience store.

He'd just passed a Walmart, though, and from the cluster of cars parked near one of its entrances, it was probably one that stayed open 24/7. Emma had looked so bedraggled and tired by the time he dropped her off that she'd probably dropped on the bed and fallen asleep.

He would take her there tomorrow... but he could also grab a few things now and leave them at the motel office, so she could at least get cleaned up in the morning. He glanced at his watch again. He had plenty of time.

It had seemed like a quick and easy task, but that was before he actually stepped inside the store. Now, blinking against the bright interior lights, he stared blankly at the sea of displays in the women's department trying to remember what his younger sister, Lacey, liked to wear. She was out in California now, married and in graduate school, and she hadn't been home in quite a while.

But she wore a lot of glitter and color, if he remembered right. Spangly things. Cartoon characters on her sweatshirts. Fluorescent-hued tennis shoes. Emma appeared to be maybe five or six years younger than his own thirty-two. Was she the glittery type when she wasn't supposedly fleeing her past?

He wandered through the clothes department, more mystified by the minute.

He shied well away from the lingerie area, and finally settled on a navy sweatshirt and matching sweatpants. She'd seemed sort of small, so that's the size he grabbed. He paused, then switched to large, remembering Lacey liked such things roomy, and added a package of gray tube socks to the cart.

After grabbing a forty-pound bag of Purina dog chow for Maisie, he went through the self-checkout line and headed out to his truck.

On his way back to the motel, he reviewed the past few hours. Not much of it made sense. He had no doubt that someone was after Emma. But was there a connection between the incident in the barn and her story about the jealous ex-boyfriend back in Ogallala? What was really going on here? Why would a young, obviously well-educated woman warrant such an effort across state lines?

If someone had wanted her dead, he would've had ample opportunity to shoot on at least a couple of occasions. So apparently she was wanted alive. But if not by the man she'd called Randy, then who?

He felt in his pocket for the knife he'd found on the alleyway floor of the sales barn, a few yards from the water spigot. He'd carefully wrapped it in tissue, and if there was a post office open on Saturday mornings around here, he would be sending it to Megan via express delivery. The stableman's story had seemed plausible, though a few minutes ago Jake had called the emergency number posted in the horse barn. The sleepy-voiced barn manager had no recollection of any employees matching the man's description, but with luck, fingerprints on the knife would yield his true identity, a rap sheet and some answers.

Jake's phone rang, breaking the predawn quiet of the hum of his tires on the highway and Maisie's quiet snoring in the backseat. Probably Uncle Oliver, up early doing chores with another theory about the missing cattle.

He lifted his phone, glanced at the screen. *Unavailable.* But surely it wasn't Emma—she must've fallen asleep the instant she hit her pillow.

"Jake." The hushed, frightened voice definitely wasn't Uncle Oliver's.

"Emma? What's wrong?"

"There's someone here. He's trying to get in. He's—" She uttered a soft cry, and then Jake heard her phone clatter against something hard.

In an instant he shifted back into full deputy mode. He floored the accelerator. Called 9-1-1.

And prayed that in this very rural area, the universal number had a chance of reaching a dispatcher *fast.*

FIVE

Staring at the open bathroom door from across the room, Emma bent down and groped for the cell phone she'd dropped, not daring to take her eyes away from the small, high bathroom window. She felt as if she were watching a rattlesnake coiling for a strike.

A prowler had furtively halted in front of her motel room. Pried at the window sash. Jiggled the doorknob. The footsteps crept away. Then she'd heard them crunching through the winter-dried weeds and snow around the corner of the building. She'd called Jake moments ago and he was on his way, but he was a good five miles off.

The bathroom window rattled again.

She drew in a shaky breath and backed up another step.

As soon as Jake had dropped her off, she'd locked herself inside this motel room with its wobbly dead bolt lock and old-fashioned safety chain.

The door itself was a flimsy hollow core model that her Grandma Lily could've kicked in without much trouble. But that kind of noise would draw attention, and the person outside obviously didn't want curious faces pressing at the front windows of the other units, or for the manager at the other end of the building to be alerted. No, he was looking for a way to quietly break in.

A manager trotting over to check things out would surely scare off the intruder and eliminate the risk of contacting the local police. A perfect scenario—

But that couldn't happen because she had no way to call the front desk.

The old rotary phone on the nightstand was dead, its sticker with the motel's name and number faded to invisibility. There wasn't a phone book in the room, no soap wrappers or scratch pads with the motel's phone number printed on them.

And dialing directory assistance apparently didn't work out here, or she could've used her cell to alert the oblivious manager who was probably dozing behind his desk.

Her only hope was Jake.

Scenes from the old classic movie *Psycho* ran through her thoughts as she cradled her cell phone in her damp palm, ready to dial 9-1-1. Dreading the complications that could arise if she did…though maybe Jake himself had already made that call.

Something tap-tap-tapped at the bathroom window, then she heard the squeal of nails and wood being pried apart. *A crowbar?*

Glass splintered. Slivers shattered on the bathroom tile.

Her hand shaking, Emma rapidly dialed 9-1-1 and talked to the dispatcher as more glass crashed to the bathroom floor.

The window was high, not much bigger than a basement casement window. It wouldn't be an easy route. But someone outside meant business and had taken cover in the darkness of the alley to break in, tired of playing it safe. If he was thin and wiry enough—like that cop who had stood in her kitchen next to Todd's body— he could probably manage to wedge himself through that window.

Please, God, tell me what to do here.

If there was just one guy, she could run out the front door and race for the motel office. If there were two, one of them could be lying in wait.

Another piece of glass shattered.

A pair of headlights swung off the highway, sent light sweeping across the curtains, then bounced and swayed as the vehicle crossed the rutted parking lot and came to a stop in front of her motel room.

Praying it was Jake, she ran to the window and drew back the curtain an inch. Blinded by the headlights, she let the curtains slip from her fingers.

From outside the bathroom window, someone yelped in pain and muttered a low, vicious curse.

Footsteps strode to her door. A dog barked. A distant siren wailed. "Emma. Are you still in there? Emma!"

Her knees turned weak with relief at the familiar voice and she flung the door open. "Someone…someone has been trying to break in. Outside—bathroom window. I called 9-1-1."

"I did, too." He gripped her shoulders. "Same drill. Get in my truck, lock the doors. I'll be back."

He hesitated a split second, until she'd climbed into his truck, and then he took off around the corner to the back of the long building with his dog at his heels.

All along the length of the motel, lights came on. Doors opened and faces peered outside. At the far end, the motel office door opened and a wizened old man hobbled out, his hands on his hips.

Even from this distance, she could see he was riled.

But what she heard clearest, from somewhere over on a side street, were the sounds of a car door slamming. An engine gunning. The squeal of tires.

And she knew the prowler was gone.

Rudy Wheeler, the overweight, sandy-haired deputy who arrived just minutes after Jake, looked more relieved than disappointed to discover that his quarry had escaped.

Now, he stood rocking on his boot heels, a clipboard in hand as he studied the broken glass. "Someone sure wanted to get in this room," he mused, eyeing

Emma. "You say he was outside quite a while."

She nodded, not meeting his eyes.

"The room is registered to me, Officer," Jake explained. "We're in town with horses consigned to the sale tomorrow."

"That so." Wheeler gave him a speculative look. "Or maybe you have something else, too, a little more pricey? Worth going after like this? We get that kind, coming through town on their way between the West Coast and Denver. We may be small town folks, but we ain't fools."

Given the man's cursory inspection of the crowbar marks on the window and how he'd veered from a break-in investigation to suspicions of drug trafficking, Jake guessed that a lot of things slipped by him.

"You're welcome to bring in a drug dog. Unless a previous guest hid something under the mattress, you won't find anything here." Jake shot a quick glance at Emma. He *hoped* that was true.

She'd claimed that a violent ex-boyfriend was after her, but had she told the truth? Could she be on the run related to some sort of drug deal gone wrong? So much crime these days stemmed from some facet of the drug trade that maybe it wasn't so far-fetched for this deputy to be giving both of them a narrowed look.

"I might just do that," Wheeler growled. "Give me your names."

The wizened hotel clerk had hovered at the deputy's elbow since he arrived. "I got all that in the motel register, Rudy," he said with obvious relish. "Address and credit card, too. Everything. You gonna arrest them?"

"So around here the police arrest the *victims?*" Jake snarled.

The clerk's eyes widened and he stepped back.

The deputy ignored him, his level gaze fixed on Jake. "Names?"

"Jake Kincaid. My friend Emma White

was in the room. I'm planning to stay out at the sales arena with the horses."

"That so. Just where are you two from?"

"I'm from Montana, south of Lost Falls. And—"

"I was raised in Montana," Emma interjected. "But I've been gone a long while. I'm in the process of moving back."

Wheeler looked back and forth between them. "Why do you suppose someone was so interested in your room instead of all the others, ma'am? You got enemies?"

"The thought makes me shudder." Stifling a yawn, she met his gaze straight on. "That end unit would be the farthest away from the security lights and other guests. Maybe some guy figured a traveler could have a lot of cash or something. But if that's what he thought, he was dead wrong."

This would be the right time to mention that ex-boyfriend who was stalking her. So why wasn't she saying anything?

And what was this about her coming from Montana?

Jake frowned at her, but she shot a warning glance back at him in return.

"It's late, Deputy. Emma had a hard day of travel and no sleep tonight, apparently. Maybe we oughta let her turn in and we can continue this tomorrow."

Wheeler flipped to his previous page of notes, then capped his pen. "That won't be necessary."

"You've got enough there to start an investigation?"

"Enough."

"Are you going to look into this? Someone damaged property, trying to break into a guest's room. Who knows what he might have done if he'd actually gotten inside?"

"I lifted a few prints out back. But with little or no evidence and no witnesses, this would be like trying to find a sparrow in the forest."

"You'll run the prints?"

"Yes, yes…I'll run the prints. But most times, nothing—"

"You'll let me know if you turn up a name?" Jake reached for the billfold in his back jeans pocket and pulled out a business card.

Wheeler drew himself up, making Jake think of a banty rooster. "That's not information we hand out to just anyone, mister."

"But for her own safety, I think Emma should at least know if this prowler is in the system, and if she's at risk."

"Yes. Well. The sheriff's office will be in touch," Wheeler blustered, heading for his patrol car. "And you're welcome to call in, if you choose."

Emma was shivering, despite the jacket she'd pulled on when they all had stepped outside. Jake dropped an arm around her shoulders and drew her close as the deputy drove away. "Well, that was useless."

"I'm just glad it's over. But what if the prowler comes back?"

"It'll be dawn in another hour. I don't think he'll try anything in broad daylight. Are you ready to turn in and try to get some sleep?"

She looked over her shoulder at the open motel room door. "Definitely not in there."

"Of course not. Hey," Jake called out to the motel clerk, who was heading back to the office. "Emma needs a different room."

"Don't have one," he called out over his shoulder.

"But there's only a few cars here."

"I don't have another room for you, and I don't want trouble. I'll tear up your registration and credit card number so you can be on your way. No charge."

"That unit next to your office doesn't look like it's in use."

The old man kept walking.

Emma touched Jake's sleeve. "It's okay. The night is nearly over anyhow. I'll just sleep in the backseat of your pickup for a while."

"Not exactly the best."

She smiled a little, but her eyes were weary and sad. "Believe me, I no longer expect that at all."

Nothing about this situation was normal. *Nothing*.

A normal, everyday person didn't stow away in a horse trailer. Find herself being assaulted in a horse barn, or have someone trying to break into her motel room an hour later.

Especially not a pretty young woman like her, who looked as though she ought to be leading a safe, quiet and ordinary suburban life with 2.5 kids and an SUV.

The past few hours had sent warning bells ringing in Jake's head, raising more questions than ever about this lovely, mysterious woman who had dropped into his life.

She'd been lying to him.

What was going on here? If that "stable hand" had been the man she'd feared, he could have quietly strangled her or snapped her neck. But there'd already been ample opportunity to kill her if someone wanted her dead.

Once again Jake thought about the possibility that for some reason she was wanted alive.

She had to have something in her possession. Know something, or have seen something she shouldn't have.

Or maybe, she'd been tangled up with the people who were pursuing her, and had done something *seriously* wrong. Betrayal could be a ticket for a death sentence.

Before he left for Montana, he was going to get to the bottom of this, or he might just be turning her over to the authorities himself.

SIX

Jake speared a bite of his bacon and cheddar cheese omelet and leveled a look at Emma over his upraised fork. "We need to have a talk."

He'd been her protector last night. He'd been kind. He'd handed her a new set of oversize sweats this morning, so she could finally change into something fresh. Though the sleeves and pant legs were all ten inches too long, she at least felt a little more human, and for that she was grateful.

But now, the cold look in his eyes made her shiver with unease. No wonder he'd chosen this booth in the far back corner of the diner. He was planning to interrogate her, and she had no idea what to say.

She nibbled a corner of her marmalade toast and tried to look unconcerned, but inside, her stomach was starting to twist into a painful knot. "What about?"

"The truth. Or as close as you can manage it."

She pulled together a smile, and hoped it looked real. "If I weren't so tired, I think I could be offended."

"Let's start with the easy ones. Like your name."

"You saw my driver's license. Your friend Megan looked me up in the legal system."

A muscle along his jawline twitched. "So why don't I believe you're really Emma White?"

Maybe because he was right. How many people stumbled over their own name? Yet she had, when they first met, because the new identity felt foreign to her tongue.

She'd always had a problem with her new names.

After all her years flying under the radar in WITSEC, she'd never gotten over her unease with living a lie; still wrestled with the half truths she'd had to tell to keep herself and her family alive.

Now only she was left, and the lies still had to continue. She was so tired of it all. But the last thing she dared do was risk confessing to a random cowboy who'd happened into her path. He'd probably figure she was lying—again—and hand her over to Rudy Wheeler.

Or worse, he might decide to play a white knight, get too involved and end up dead.

She took a sip of her coffee. "What else?"

"You implied that you'd never been to Montana when we were talking in the horse barn. Yet you told Deputy Wheeler you were raised there."

"I didn't say I'd never *been* there. I just

said that your part of the state was probably beautiful. I'm sure I haven't seen all
of Montana."

"You had a chance to tell the deputy
about that guy back at the truck stop in
Ogallala. Why didn't you? Either you're
the unluckiest woman on the planet, or
every bit of this is related."

She forced herself to take another bite
of toast, wishing she dared trust him, yet
knowing it wouldn't be fair to him if she
told him too much.

"Well?"

The danger of revealing her identity
to anyone had been drummed into her
since she was nine years old. She closed
her eyes, willing away the images of her
father lying facedown in a widening pool
of blood. Her mother's broken body at the
scene of the car accident. Maybe she'd felt
as if she were acting in some endless play
all these years, but to her enemies it was
definitely no joke.

"You're a nice guy, Jake. I desperately

needed to escape back in Ogallala. You were handy. But I don't want to involve you in my problems. If you could just drop me off near a bus stop in Denver after the sale, I can—"

"I was a deputy, remember?"

She had to smile at that. "I would've gathered that anyway, from your conversation with your friend Megan."

"I'm probably a better bet than some cross-country bus." He studied her intently. "But I'm also not going to let a fugitive slip through my fingers. Tell me what's going on, or I'll be tempted to let the local police figure you out."

A middle-aged waitress cruised up to the booth with a coffeepot in hand. "Refills?"

Jake nodded and watched her top off their coffee cups, then idly stirred the creamer into his own cup as he watched the waitress work her way around the room. When she was well out of hearing range, he turned his attention back to Emma. "So. The cops, or me?"

Neither, but he had no idea what he was asking of her. "When do you expect your friend's horses will sell?"

He watched her with the lazy intensity of a cat studying its prey. "Midafternoon. Why?"

"I don't want to talk here. It's not safe. But when we leave the sales grounds, I'll tell you what you need to know. Okay?"

"I'd rather know right now."

Her palms turned damp. She swallowed. "Then I—"

A half-dozen cowboys came in the front door of the little diner, bringing with them the scents of horse, hay and sawdust. The waitress waved them to the back and they headed for the table next to the back booth, spurs jangling and chair legs screeching against the old wood flooring as they settled at the table.

Their arrival was a reprieve...but not for long.

Now she just needed to decide if she should disappear during the sale, or if she dared gamble on Jake Kincaid.

It was definitely time for another prayer.

The cavernous horse barn had been deserted last night, a place filled with dark shadows and a menacing air.

Now, the place was nearly impassable. Horses were cross-tied in the aisles; their owners busy brushing, clipping, spraying them with aerosol shine, daubing black shoe polish on neatly trimmed hooves.

Buyers gathered in swarms around some of the animals, shooting questions at the handlers, jockeying for a better view. In the aisle not blockaded by cross-tied horses, other animals were being led to and from the heated shower stalls, or were saddled and heading for the indoor arena.

It was a sea of Western hats and boots and silver belt buckles the size of dinner plates, and there were kids and dogs and baby strollers everywhere.

Emma followed Jake to his two stalls, where a half-dozen women in lean-cut jeans and a few rancher-type men were studying the mares through the vertical metal bars of the stalls with sale catalogs in hand. Emma stayed back, watching him charm them all as he fielded questions, his ready grin deepening the vertical slashes bracketing his mouth.

"I'd like to see the sorrel under saddle," one of the women said. "If you've got the time."

Jake nodded, pulled the mare out of the stall and cross-tied her. "She did really well in the reining futurities last year. Earned around fifty grand with limited hauling, and she's sound as a dollar. Guaranteed. She's ready to go out and win big for someone."

Everyone looked down at the sales catalog they held open to the mare's description.

He hauled a saddle out of the next stall down, settled a neoprene pad and Navajo blanket on the mare's back, then saddled her, keeping up a steady stream of answers as a crowd grew.

Like an equine version of the Pied Piper, he led the mare down the aisle to the indoor arena with the potential buyers following. Emma fell in behind them.

"I don't know much about horses, but this seems like a good one," she said to a woman at her left who held a toddler in her arms.

The blonde nodded. "My husband is interested, but I doubt we have a chance at her. The horses Kincaid chooses to train and show are exceptional."

Emma glanced down at the catalog she'd picked up at the front door. "I thought the mare was from out east somewhere. Isn't Kincaid from Montana?"

The woman laughed. "You *must* be new at this. He's known from coast to coast, and people send him training horses from all over the country. He showed this mare to a championship last year."

Emma blinked. "I thought he was a deputy sheriff."

"I heard he was, but then something terrible…" Her voice trailed off, and bright flags of color bloomed in her cheeks. "Well, anyway, he quit a while back to ranch and train horses full-time. The rest is just hearsay so I have no business repeating it. Good luck, if you're planning to bid on either of the mares he brought."

The woman darted away and was soon lost in the crowd.

Something terrible? Something that he'd had to deal with—or could it be something that he'd done? Emma frowned to herself as she entered the indoor area. Maybe she wasn't the only one with secrets.

The air was far chillier out here. She followed a stream of people moving up into the bleachers and settled down to watch the carousel of colorful horses jogging and loping along the rail, some going in the opposite directions, while in the vast open center, a number of riders were tuning up their horses with spins and sliding stops.

Jake led the mare into a quiet spot, checked the girth, then swung easily into the saddle. The mare stood statue-still as he shook considerable slack into the reins, then knotted the ends and draped them over the saddle horn.

"Lookee there, Martha," a man chortled from behind Emma's row. He leaned forward to point at Jake. "In the center. Isn't that Jake Kincaid out there?"

"What's he thinking, with no reins out in that mess of horses?" The disapproving tone was that of an older woman.

Emma leaned forward, unable to tear her gaze away as Jake gave the mare some sort of invisible signal. She walked forward, her head low, and began jogging in a circle.

One by one, the other riders in the center of the arena melted away to the perimeter rail as Jake's mare broke into an easy lope for a few circles, sped into a run for another few, then dropped back into a molasses slow lope again. What the signals were Emma couldn't even fathom because Jake hadn't touched the reins even once.

The sorrel's circles tightened, and suddenly she started spinning into 360s, her mane flying, her rear-end planted firmly in one spot. She stopped, reversed and spun again, then halted. She stood stock-still for a few heartbeats, then she took off at a dead run, buried her hindquarters into the ground and did a sliding stop, leaving a perfectly parallel set of thirty-foot skid marks behind. Jake had never once touched the reins.

Applause and cheers roared from the bleachers, and Emma stared in wonder as Jake stepped off the mare and led her out of the arena. What kind of endless, careful training did something like that take? She couldn't begin to imagine.

Patches, the childhood pony she'd shared with her sister before they were orphaned and everything in their young lives had gone so horribly wrong, had happily veered toward low tree limbs to knock off his little passengers. He'd suddenly put on the brakes, watch them tumble to the ground, then he'd contentedly start grazing. He'd balked at going to the end of the driveway without considerable persuasion.

Horses definitely had a mind of their own, but the one Jake had just ridden had seemed likc a seamless extension of his thoughts, willing to do anything based on the most invisible cues. That sort of bond didn't happen if someone was impatient, rough or cruel.

Whatever doubts she had about trusting him with her most dangerous secrets, this new glimpse into his character had put at least a few of them to rest.

She sidestepped down her bleacher row to the stairway at the end, and headed back into the milling crowd in the horse barn. It was even harder to make it through the crowd now that an announcer's voice was blaring over the loudspeaker system, urging bidders to go to the pavilion housing the auction ring.

Someone jostled her from behind, making her stumble.

She barely regained her balance...then the crowd shifted, flowing like a river around a horse tied in the aisle, knocking her into a stall door. A knee caught the back of her own and her leg buckled instantly, nearly dropping her to the floor.

She took a sharp breath and instantly her skin prickled with uneasy awareness at a familiar, cloying odor. Sweat, mingled with cheap aftershave. Just like the man who'd grabbed her in the barn.

The stable hand who might not have been a stable hand at all, no matter what he'd told Jake.

Fear rushed through her as she plowed ahead, slipping between the people crowding toward a side entrance in the barn marked Sales Arena.

There were people all around. Nothing

could happen to her here. Could it? Had she just imagined that scent because of her moment of panic?

"Hey!" A hand settled on her shoulder, nearly stopping her heart.

She spun around and found Jake studying her. "You look like you've seen a ghost. Anything wrong?"

"For starters, you scared me half to death."

"I was just trying to catch you before you walked on by. I thought we'd better touch base before I lost you again." His faint grin flickered, faded. "You are one jumpy woman, though I guess you have good cause."

She looked over his shoulder and recognized the sorrel mare standing in a stall, still saddled. She edged closer to the stall, away from the people passing by. "I—I didn't even see you. Crowds make me a little nervous."

"I don't have to wonder why. I'm still looking forward to our talk, by the way."

And I'm looking forward to getting out of here. The sooner the better. "When will you be done?"

"Rough guess would be around four, based on my lot numbers. I'll stay here by the stalls until the mares go in, so I can answer questions. Afterward, I'll be ready to go as soon as I can settle up at the office."

Six long hours? She felt herself pale.

"You ought to go in now and watch the bidding. It can be pretty entertaining, especially when there's so much money flying from up in those bleachers."

"I don't think—"

"Go on. There's a big crowd, it's well lit. The bleachers surround three sides of the auction ring so no one could sneak up on you in there. You might even have some fun."

Fun. Now *there* was a foreign concept.

There'd been no siblings in her adoptive home. No cousins that she knew of. Friendships in the various towns had been discouraged, as she and her new parents moved from place to place because a little girl might say too much.

A frisson of excitement tingled through her.

Her new life was starting, and soon everything would be different. She could have friends again. Go where she wanted to, do what she wanted, and not have to look over her shoulder.

It would make no sense to slip away from Jake just yet. All she had to do was make it to the Montana mountains with him, and then she could disappear into her next and final new identity.

Jake surely wouldn't bother to track her down.

She was just an inconvenience; an unexpected bit of baggage that he'd picked up on the way.

Though if it was all so perfectly planned, why did the thought of leaving him behind already make her feel sad?

SEVEN

Emma curled up on a bale of hay in a corner of the spare stall Jake used to store his equipment and supplies, pulled a paperback out of her purse and tried to read.

With the nonstop, rapid-fire chant of the auctioneer coming from the sales ring and the hollow clip-clop of hooves going up and down the cement aisle, she finally gave up on trying to concentrate and just leaned her head against the wall.

Now and then someone would stop by to ask Jake questions and she found herself listening intently, completely adrift over the vernacular.

What was a flat-kneed lope?

A lunge line prospect, or a breeding stock paint mare?

It was an entirely different language, fascinating and confusing and—she had to admit—all the more interesting because of Jake's smooth, deep voice. Its warm tones seemed to wrap around her, making her feel safe and protected, just because he was out there, a few feet away.

But she'd better not plan to depend on him, that was for sure.

He was now the one link with her past; the one person who knew she was on the run and heading west. Once she managed to escape her pursuers and then left him behind in Deer Lodge, she'd be free and clear of any connection to her life in Chicago. With her new identity she would buy a decent used car, then completely disappear.

He rapped on the stall door. "The sorrel is on deck, so I've got to go. Are you coming?"

Emma scrambled to her feet and dusted off the bits of hay clinging to her pants. "Can I?"

"You can come with me to the gate, then step off to the side while they auction the mare." He tightened the girth on the mare's saddle. "After she goes through the ring, I'll have to exit the opposite side, but you can just double back and meet me here."

Emma followed Jake and the mare to an entrance gate where horses and owners were lining up. "Are you nervous?"

He smiled down at her. "Nope."

"Do you think she'll go for a lot?"

"I hope so, for George's sake."

"Her owner?"

Jake nodded. "He's been struggling to keep his ranch, after having a lot of setbacks this past year or so. Good prices on his mares could make all the difference."

From a stand overlooking the sales ring, the auctioneer banged his gavel and shouted "Sold!" and the horses in line moved up, leaving Jake just outside the ring.

Emma stepped up to the rail and peered at the crowd. The bleachers in here were steep, completely packed with people, and they went clear to the rafters, like an amphitheater in microcosm. "Wow."

The rapid patter of the auctioneer rose and fell as the three ringmen paced the sides of the fenced auction ring scouting the crowd for bids—cajoling, begging, teasing—then screaming "Yes!" when they found one.

She found herself searching the bleachers row by row, wondering if the man who'd tried to grab her was here now, like any other ordinary, law-abiding citizen.

"Sold! To bidder number eight-five, up on the right."

Jake swung up into the saddle, ducked his head under a low beam and rode the sorrel into the arena.

The auctioneer read a description of the mare's breeding and accomplishments, then started off the bidding at twenty-five hundred. As the bidding rose, the ringmen erupted in shouts of "Yes! Yes! Yes!" as they fielded bids from the crowd.

Emma watched Jake, feeling oddly pleased and proud when he dropped the mare's reins and sent her into spins in both directions that turned the two of them into a blur of man and horseflesh.

The hushed crowd burst into a renewed flurry of bidding, and Emma felt herself swept into the excitement, half understanding what the auctioneer was saying. Jake looked so tall, dark and elegant on a horse that she wished she had a camera just so she could remember the moment always.

The bang of the gavel made her jump.

"Sold! Thirty-eight-five. Oak Creek Farms, number twenty-seven."

Back at the stall, Jake was already unsaddling the sorrel and getting ready to tack up the other horse when Emma arrived. She beamed at him. "Wow, nearly four grand. That's good, isn't it?"

He turned the mare into her stall and slipped off her bridle. He came out of the stall grinning. "It would be, for a lesser mare. You need to add a zero, there."

Her mouth dropped open. "No."

"Yep—almost forty grand. The other one is her younger full sister, so she ought to do pretty well herself, too."

"I had no idea. Absolutely none."

"They aren't all worth that much. But when you get a real keeper you hang on to her, work with her, give her endless attention and help her reach her full potential."

There was a faraway look in his eyes and Emma wondered if he was still talking about horses, or was he thinking about someone important in his life, like a wife or a fiancée. If so, she was one very lucky woman.

Jake had the truck and trailer hitched up already, and parked near the exit. By the time the auction of both mares was over and settled, it was a little after four, though there were nearly fifty lots left to auction and the parking lot was still full.

"Good guess on the time," Emma said, looking at the clock on the dashboard of the truck. She watched the road behind them in the side mirror while Jake followed a winding two-lane highway for a few miles, then veered onto a freeway entrance.

"I figured we'd drive a while before we pull off for supper. Is that all right?" Jake flicked a glance in the rearview mirror, then settled into the right lane of the freeway and set the cruise control at sixty-five. "I haven't seen anyone follow us, have you?"

"No. Not that I can tell." Maybe it was really all over. The running, the fear. The frightening possibility that she could be set up for Todd's murder and sent back to Chicago to face false accusations that would be nearly impossible to fight.

"Penny for your thoughts."

She knew he meant her entire sordid past. She felt her eyes burn as she looked out the side window and watched the flatlands speed by to the east. The housing developments north of Denver were thinning out now, interspersed among pastures with horses and cattle clustered around hay feeders out in the snow.

"Do any of the people out here know how lucky they are?" She glanced wearily at Jake, then fixed her gaze on the ribbon of freeway unfolding ahead, far as the eye could see. Here and there, an exit sign appeared and offered a trip to a town whose name she didn't recognize. "I try to imagine living an ordinary life, in one of the ordinary houses in a small town. A place where no one knows my name beyond the town limits, and no one else cares. It sounds like luxury to me."

"Some of those people might say they're bored."

"But they have no idea how wonderful that is. If they just make the effort, they can choose to do something different, be someone else. Their lives haven't been mapped out by a terrible event that changed everything forever."

"What happened, Emma?"

Her throat felt thick. Old, remembered anxiety crawled across her skin and fragments of her mom's warnings came back to her. *Don't ever tell. Never, ever tell, Emma. Do you understand how dangerous it would be? Do you want someone to come hurt us?* She started to shake, just as she had when she was nine, whenever her dad shook his finger in front of her face and reminded her, over and over and over.

Jake had helped her. Protected her. But he had no idea of what he was dealing with, and she couldn't let him risk his life without telling him the truth. Yet, would it be worse for him if he knew too much?

"Emma? We've got thirteen hours ahead of us, so there's plenty of time."

"Honestly, I'm thankful for the ride.

You've been very kind. But I've known you for less than two days, and I'm just a hitchhiker. I'm not sure it's a good idea to tell you anything."

"Except for one small problem."

She pinned her gaze on him, suddenly wary. *What if he'd been sent to intercept her?* Though on second thought, that made little sense. She could've chosen any vehicle at that truck stop, not just his. "What problem?"

"I may not be in law enforcement any longer, but I believe in the law. Harboring a fugitive or aiding and abetting a criminal is hardly part of my game plan these days."

"You already had that sheriff check me out."

"Using the name you gave me."

"Then just let me out anywhere and you'll be done with me."

He sighed. "Would I? Then I'd have to assume the worst, contact the local sheriff and turn you in. And I'd have to stick around and make a statement—maybe more, and I just don't have time. I've got to get back to my ranch as soon as I can."

"Then drop me off and be on your way. I promise I won't tell on you for letting a hardened criminal escape."

He laughed at that. "No, I don't imagine you would."

They drove in silence for a few miles. "Hungry?"

Just the word made her stomach growl. "I'm fine."

"Yeah, right. Up ahead is the last fast-food place for a good long while. Are you game for McDonald's?"

She gave up her pretense when her stomach growled again and he shot a sidelong, knowing look at her. "I'm game for just about anything they've got."

The trailer wouldn't fit under the eaves of the drive-through, so they both went inside, where Jake stood in line for the order and Emma slipped into the bathroom to wash up as best she could.

On their way back out to the truck, she stared longingly at a Walmart next door and mentally counted what was left of her limited cash. "Would you mind?"

"Are you going to disappear in there?"

"Nope. And I'll be quick, promise."

She wolfed her Quarter Pounder and fries on the way over to the store parking lot, then raced into the store while Jake finished eating in the truck.

Basic toiletries, mascara and blusher were quick decisions. In the clothing section she lingered a little longer, tossing packages of cotton underwear, three pairs of jeans, a couple of shirts, pajamas and a sweater into the cart. It was a good start on the future, symbolic of her new life. She could hardly wait to shower and change— maybe at a truck stop along the way that offered those facilities to long-haul truckers.

Feeling lighter and more carefree than

she had in a long time, she walked out of the store with her bags in hand.

The truck and trailer were gone.

EIGHT

Emma stared out at the parking lot, her heart sinking. Jake had probably been hoping for a good moment to leave her behind, and she'd handed it to him on a silver platter. She felt a twinge in her heart, knowing Jake had driven right out of her life without a second thought, but she could hardly blame him.

Not when she'd debated about quietly slipping away in the same manner.

She moved to one side of the entrance and leaned against the gray brick wall, dropping her overflowing shopping bags at her feet. *What now?*

Her plan had been a good one, until the incident in Ogallala. Taking the bus to Deer Lodge had been a far better option than flying or driving her own SUV, for the sake of anonymity, and her three-hundred-dollar junker of a temporary car wouldn't have made it that far.

Once in Deer Lodge, she'd planned to find the post office and pick up the registered package she'd sent to herself, which included documentation for her new life as Jeanne Martin, including a credit card and a bank card in that name so she could access all of her savings.

But it was all waiting for her in Deer Lodge, not here, and rather than risk carrying a lot of money, she'd planned on just enough cash to cover her travel days. *If* things had gone according to plan.

Daring to ask the help of a stranger had been a risky thing to do, but she'd been running for her life and desperate. Now, in the bright light of day, the prospect of taking that risk all over again was too frightening to even consider. Would the clerk at the customer service counter know if there was a cross-country bus stop in this town?

She grabbed the handles of her bags and wearily turned to go back into the store, her hastily eaten lunch now sitting in her stomach like a twenty-pound lead weight.

"Hey, lady," a deep voice drawled. "Need a ride?"

She stopped in her tracks. Turned, and found Jake behind her with Maisie on a leash.

"I might just be heading the right way."

Her heart lifted at the sight of his half smile and the faint twinkle in those warm, chocolate eyes. "I—I thought you'd left."

"I did. I went to fill up the gas tank, then parked at the end of the parking lot so I could walk Maisie." He lifted a shoulder. "My mom and sister can stay in stores for days, so I figured I had time."

"You did, actually. I just came outside." She ducked her head to hide the pathetic tsunami of relief rushing through her, coupled with the realization of how much she would've missed him if he'd gone.

She followed him to the side of the building, where he'd parked the truck and trailer in an empty section of the parking lot, and tossed her bags into the backseat, then climbed in the front.

Guilt seeped into her heart at the trouble she'd put him through. Yet all he'd asked of her was the truth, and even though she'd refused, he'd still come back for her.

If he was going to put his life on the line for her, he deserved to know.

Suddenly nervous, she studied her folded hands as she waited for him to get behind the wheel.

"I guess we need to talk," she said quietly. "It's only fair, given the danger I've put you through."

He draped his left wrist on the top of the steering wheel and pivoted in his seat. "You were the apparent target. Not me."

"True, but you tried to protect me. I

never expected that, and I want you to know that I'm thankful."

"But you're obviously in some kind of serious trouble." He regarded her with a troubled expression. "And I'd guess it's not over."

"You have no idea."

"Maybe there's something I can do. But you have to trust me, Emma."

She choked back a laugh. "If only it were that simple. The crazy thing is that the truth is far more unbelievable than the lies."

"Try me."

She pensively twisted the leather fringe on her purse around her index finger, wondering where to start. "A very long story short, my sister and I did grow up in Montana, like I said. We were orphaned when Kris was ten and I was seven. I don't know what happened to her, but I was adopted a year later and taken out east. My parents—adoptive parents—were good people."

"But they're gone now, too?"

Emma nodded. "We were in Washington, D.C., one spring when I was twelve, and we witnessed a murder in a parking garage. It was a hit on a United States senator, ordered by the powerful Rodriguez drug cartel. It was *horrible* for that poor man, but it also changed our lives forever."

"Did you have to testify?"

"We all did. With the promise of protection afterward."

His eyes widened. "You've been in witness protection all this time?"

She nodded. "Eduardo Rodriguez has been on death row for years. He put out a contract on my family in revenge right after the trial, so we had no choice. A number of his lieutenants just got between fifteen to twenty years."

"So some of them are back on the streets now."

"Exactly. And even behind bars, Rodriguez is a powerful man." She swallowed hard. "My mom was killed in a 'car accident' last year. We were moved right afterward, but then someone managed to discover our new location just two weeks ago. It wasn't pretty."

"Your dad?"

"Sniper, grocery store parking lot at night." She heaved a sigh. "I started planning to disappear on my own after Dad was killed because I no longer trusted our contact or anyone above him. Then I came home and discovered him dead on my kitchen floor Wednesday night, and two men discussing how they were going to pin his death on me."

He eyed her thoughtfully. "So there was never a crazed ex-boyfriend after you, then."

"No. I just didn't want to reveal that whole awful mess to a stranger and put you in danger. Besides, who would believe it? What I don't understand is why they didn't just shoot me, too. I'm a jogger, so there was ample opportunity."

Staring out the windshield, Jake

drummed his fingers on the top of the steering wheel. "Good question."

"So you see? The truth is stranger than the stories I told to mask it. Believe what you will."

"What about your sister? Are you hoping to find her?"

"I don't know if she's even alive or where she is. The WITSEC rules are that you never, ever contact anyone from your past, for their safety as well as yours. I never so much as tried to look her up on Google or check on Facebook, for fear that the wrong people would find out."

He nodded, still staring at the snowy landscape beyond the parking lot. "Do you think she's near the town of Deer Lodge?"

"No, not at all. It was just along the bus route, and I figured it was as good a place as any to simply disappear."

"Hmm." He shot a glance at her. "Interesting that you've been in WITSEC fifteen years, but all of this violence has happened in the last year or so, instead of right after the trial. Someone like Rodriguez usually metes out swift retribution as warning to underlings about keeping their mouths shut, and as a show of force to his enemies. Why now, instead of years ago? What changed?"

"I—I don't know. A lot of his friends are out of prison now, but he sure didn't need to wait on them. With his money and power, he could have hired someone to do his dirty work."

She'd held in her emotions since her father's death, caught up in the horror of his murder, her fears and her frantic plans to escape. But whether it was Jake's calming presence or the fact that she'd shared her past for the first time, she felt rare tears stinging against her eyelids. She willed them away, impatient with her own weakness.

Jake reached over and settled his hand over hers. "It's hard enough to lose a parent, but violent circumstances like this must be a hundred times worse. I'm sorry about your loss, Emma."

She managed a faint wobbly smile. "Thanks. But don't worry about getting any more involved than you already are. Just drop me at Deer Lodge, and you can be on your way."

"Nope."

Startled, she did a double take at the firm line of his mouth. "No?"

He turned the key in the ignition and the truck engine roared to life. "It isn't a good idea. So I think I'll just take you home."

NINE

Emma stared at him. "What do you mean, 'take me home'? There's no way I'm going back to Chicago, so if that's your idea, then let me out of this truck right now."

"Not Chicago. My ranch."

Her mouth dropped open. This was not going well *at all*. "I can't go there. I have to go to Deer Lodge."

"Why? You said yourself that it was just a bus stop you chose at random. So choose a different town. False Lake, for instance. Where you'd know at least one person who is concerned about you. Me."

"Because." She cringed, knowing she

sounded like a petulant kindergartner. "Because…I may have told you the truth about me, but that doesn't change my plans."

"Just *'because'*?" He rolled his eyes. "That's certainly sound logic."

"I've got…I've got things waiting for me there. Important things."

"What? I thought you'd never been there."

"Things. Boxes I mailed ahead."

"Your safety is more important than that. If you sent clothes, you can always buy more."

"Documents. Family mementoes. It's all I have left now. Things that are treasures, but only to me." Plus the keys to her new identity and thus, to her future, though he didn't need to know that. "If I don't pick it all up, they'll eventually send it to my old return address, and then I'll never get it back." Worse, if the wrong people saw those boxes on her doorstep, they'd have an idea of where she'd headed.

"You could contact the post office and have them forward it all to False Lake."

"It's registered mail, requiring my signature."

"Then talk to the False Lake postmistress. Doris is an old doll, and knows me well. I'm sure you could show her your ID and she'd arrange things."

"But—"

"This can't be the first time that registered mail had to be forwarded. Everything will be fine."

She glanced at his strong, chiseled profile, and the implacable set of his jaw. It wasn't only the registered package that worried her now. It was the fact that she felt more and more drawn to this man who was so determined to help her...yet there was no way it could ever work out.

The longer she stayed, the greater the guarantee that she'd be headed for certain heartbreak—and the greater the chance that Jake could be in danger, too.

"Why would you want to take me to your ranch?"

"You're looking to disappear. What better place than the middle of five thousand acres, with the closest town twenty miles away?" He glanced in the rearview mirror, then fixed his gaze on the long, empty stretch of highway ahead. "False Lake has a grand total of two thousand-twenty people, give or take a few. As far as any of your nasty 'friends' know, you'll have dropped off the face of the planet. But if they do show up, I figure it will be easier to isolate and eliminate them on my own turf."

"You're scaring me, Jake."

"You *should* be scared about the guys who are after you. Just give yourself a little time here. Then you can take off again, and not be afraid someone is still breathing down your neck."

"But—"

"It's just an idea, but it's a good one. You wouldn't be on your own, jumping at shadows. And in case you're wondering, I'm not the only one who lives there. My uncle Oliver and his son, Lane, live in the main house. Oliver was Dad's partner for years, so he's a part-owner. We also have Ed Feezer, a ranch hand who comes out and works for us now and then. You won't see him much, unless he comes in for dinner."

"Oh." She stared at the snowy landscape, considering.

"A stranger in town will stand out like a bull on an ice rink. Same thing at the ranch—the dogs and Lane's goose are the best alarm system you ever saw. When a stranger shows up out there, you'd think World War III was starting."

"A *goose?*"

Jake snorted. "Believe me, Gilbert is the *last* thing you'd want to encounter in the dark. He's sneaky, and he's fierce. He totally intimidates the bull, and he has taken after me a time or two. But Lane loves him to death."

"So I could leave anytime."

"I don't plan to hold you prisoner, Emma. I'm just trying to help."

"I can't go long without a job, so it couldn't be for long. But what would your neighbors think, if some strange woman moved in? Or your...your girlfriend? Wife?"

"That's currently not an issue, but thanks for the concern." He drummed his fingers on the steering wheel, apparently lost in thought for a few miles. "My aunt passed on last year. She was a wonderful cook, and since then, Oliver and I have been just winging it in the kitchen. We could say you've been hired on as a cook and house-keeper. You do know how to cook, right?"

"Passably."

"Then you're better than the two of us put together. We'd pay you, of course, meals and lodging included."

It sounded better by the minute, though he was forgetting one important thing.

"A lot of people saw the two of us together at the sale. It wouldn't have been hard for someone to figure out which truck was yours, and copy down the license plate. I could bring trouble straight to your door."

"Let me worry about that, Emma. Please, let Oliver and me keep you safe for a while. You don't have to try to face this alone."

A shadow crossed his face, as if he were remembering some great sadness in his past, and Emma recalled the words of the blonde back at the sales arena. *I heard he was a deputy sheriff, but something terrible...*

The woman had hurried away before finishing her sentence, as if she'd been hesitant to say too much, but Jake Kincaid was definitely proving to be a surprising, complex man. What tragedy had he faced? Did the guilt and sorrow haunt him?

She might have still resisted his generous offer, but his words touched her heart. For the past two weeks she'd been totally alone, and that would be her future, too. What would it hurt to accept Jake's hospitality for a little while, and not feel she had to watch her back every moment?

"All right—maybe a week or two. And then I'll have to go."

Hundreds of miles of highway disappeared beneath the truck's wheels as Jake drove deeper into Wyoming toward Montana. Darkness had fallen several hours ago, and now the surrounding terrain was pitch-black, save for the swath of his headlights slicing through the night.

He glanced over at the woman dozing next to him, and felt a touch of tenderness warm a corner of his cold and jaded heart.

He was already notorious at the ranch for picking up strays and bringing them home, but this was one he wouldn't live down anytime soon. There'd be the usual good-natured teasing, but there would also be the knowing looks and none-too-subtle suggestions that maybe he ought to take another stab at settling down so he could finally enjoy true marital bliss.

That was an oxymoron if he'd ever heard one. And after Maura's affair and abrupt departure to marry a neighboring rancher, it wasn't something he'd be risking again for a long, *long* time.

He'd inwardly rolled his eyes when Emma began her implausible tale, knowing that she'd already flirted with the truth more times than not. He'd already started to figure that she was as dishonest as his ex-wife, but by the time she finished, he was sold. She knew too much about the WITSEC program. Her story rang true.

Except for the part about the sudden, vengeful attacks starting fourteen years after the congressman's murder. *Fourteen years.* Rodriguez had had no need to wait on a lieutenant's prison release to exact punishment upon the family whose testimony helped put him behind bars. So why so long?

The easy answer was that WITSEC was famously successful at protecting those in the program. The U.S. Marshals were certainly highly trained, dedicated people. Unless a person under their care happened to sabotage his own safety, the system worked remarkably well.

Perhaps someone in the system had gone rogue and betrayed Emma's family—perhaps for more money than he or she had ever dreamed of. But what Jake was thinking right now was a far stronger possibility. There were still people he could contact, favors he could call in from his old life. He would do it for Emma's sake… even if it broke her heart to find out the truth. And for his own sake, too, a last chance for redemption.

His unbelievable failure three years ago was still the stuff of nightmares, second guesses and sleepless nights, and there was no way to ever make it right.

But he wasn't going to fail someone again.

* * *

Emma stirred, stretched and straightened up in her seat. The clock on the dashboard said two o'clock, and unbroken night surrounded them.

Lit only by the glow of the instrument panel, Jake's five-o'clock shadow darkened his strong jaw. He looked rather like a pirate, she mused, but she kept the thought to herself.

"We must be getting close," she murmured. "Though I don't see even a single light out there."

"It would've been thirteen hours to Deer Lodge, then another four to the ranch. But since we're going straight to False Lake it should take just another hour."

She shifted uneasily. "I hope this isn't a mistake."

"If you decide it is, no problem. I think there's a Greyhound bus that goes through a town thirty miles east of us and you can catch it whenever you like."

"What is your uncle going to say about you dragging home a complete stranger?"

Jake grinned. "Make him dinner and he'll be thrilled. No questions asked."

"Um…you do have some cookbooks out there or access to the internet, right?"

"This may be cowboy country, but yep—we've got wireless."

"Good." She sank back against the seat in relief. "Between YouTube how-to videos and the online recipe sites, I should be okay, then."

"You're kidding. *YouTube?*"

"You'd be surprised at what you can learn there. I've lived alone since college, and rarely had guests. Cooking has never been much of a priority."

"You went to college?"

"Library science. Until a few days ago, I worked in a little suburban library. How about you?"

"Pre-vet, and I have a degree in biology, but that's as far as I got. I had to come back to the ranch when my dad had a heart attack. After a couple years he was strong again and I got restless, so I went into law enforcement."

"What about the horses?"

"I've always trained on the side, no matter where I was. But when Dad died, my mom couldn't handle things alone. So I'm back at the ranch for good, and I guess I've found that it's what I like best."

"So she lives with you, too?"

"Just summers. Otherwise, she has a condo in Arizona with my aunt. Those two gals might be retired, but they do volunteer work practically full-time and can run circles around anyone half their age."

The pride and love in his voice was unmistakable, and Emma felt a little twinge in her heart. What would it be like to still have a mom to confide in? To share events with, big and small, and to know that someone still loved you unequivocally, with all her heart? "Your mom sounds amazing."

He looked over at her, his eyes warm

with compassion. "I'm sorry about all you've lost, Emma. It must be tough."

She nodded. "Thanks for skipping the usual platitudes about God's will, or about how my parents are in a better place. Maybe it's true, but if God really loved people, couldn't He have spared one of my parents for a while longer? I've lost four, and that must be a record."

"I know it's hard. But I don't believe God chooses to give us tragedies. I think He mourns with us, and wants us to talk to Him in prayer. He answers those prayers in amazing ways sometimes because He wants to give us peace and comfort and strength."

Surprised, she looked at him. "Sounds like you're a strong believer."

"I am. I can't help but believe, when I've seen His hand in my life so often." He lifted his shoulder. "Believe me, I've had my share of bad times, and what I saw as a deputy sometimes made me question the entire human race. But I choose to believe in the light, not the darkness."

They fell into companionable silence as the miles rolled by unmarked by exits or towns or even a single twinkling light somewhere out on the landscape, as evidence of inhabitation.

Jake pointed out into the darkness. "Almost there."

She squinted out the window, trying to see any possible variation in the vast, black nothingness. "How in the world can you tell?"

"It's home," he said simply. "We'll go straight to the ranch because it's so late. I can show you around town another day."

The land had been becoming steadily more hilly over the past hour. Sure enough, an exit sign marked County Road 73 appeared over the next rise.

Jake slowed, veered off the highway, then headed out on an asphalt two-lane road that wound through hills and valleys. Emma leaned forward, trying to make out the terrain, but only caught glimpses of sagebrush, low, wiry trees and an occasional rocky wall rising along the side of the road. "How far now?"

"Twenty minutes."

When he finally turned onto a dusty gravel road, she felt her heart lift with anticipation. "I'll bet this country is beautiful in the daylight."

"It is. We're in the shadow of the Rockies to the west and north, the foothills to the south and east. Good ranch land for raising cattle and horses and it's also easy on the eyes."

The truck and trailer rattled and shook over the gravel road, and when Jake finally pulled to a stop beneath a high security light, Emma could still feel the rough motion in her bones, even after she stepped out of the truck. Jake opened the back door for Maisie, who ran in merry circles at being home. A large black lab appeared out of the shadows of a large barn and uttered a single woof, then bounded over to Jake with its tail wagging.

"My welcoming committee," he said with a laugh. "Looks like everyone else is asleep."

She could make out the faint outline of a long, cabinlike building next to the barn. To the left, there appeared to be a sprawling two-story house set back in the trees.

He grabbed a duffel bag out of the bed of the pickup. "Can you carry your things?"

"My fancy luggage? Sure." She reached for her shopping bags and followed him toward the house.

"Oliver, Lane and I all have the main floor bedrooms. You can have one of the rooms upstairs. There's a bathroom up there, too, with linens in the closet. So make yourself at home."

A porch light blazed on. A door squealed, and then a tall slender man stepped out on the porch. "That you, Jake?"

"Finally."

The other man hobbled to the edge of the porch. "Good, because we've got trouble, Jake. *Big* trouble. And I'm just glad you're home."

TEN

Oliver's eyed widened when he caught sight of the woman following Jake into the house. "I didn't know you were bringing company," he said gruffly, tightening the belt of his old plaid robe.

Jake stepped aside. "Emma White, this is my uncle, Oliver Kincaid."

Oliver pursed his lips, looking between Jake and Emma. "I don't believe I've heard you talk about this young lady."

"We just met," Emma said. She extended her arm and shook his hand. "Jake offered me a job on a trial basis."

Oliver raised a bushy eyebrow. "As a

ranch hand? You look mighty delicate for this kind of work, ma'am."

"As a cook and housekeeper," Jake interjected. "There's a little more to it than that, but we can talk later."

The doubt in Oliver's eyes didn't lessen. "A housekeeper and a cook, eh? Are you a *good* cook?"

"I try."

"Humph. Breakfast is at 7:00 a.m. sharp around here because Lane has to leave for school and the rest of us have chores. I'll be mighty happy about having a nice hot breakfast again. Jake, do you want to show her the guest rooms, or should I?"

"I'll do it." Jake picked up one of her shopping bags. "But I'll be right back because it sounds like you and I need to talk."

Jake led the way through the great room to the large country-style kitchen, then up the back staircase to the second floor, pointing out the three bedrooms and the bathroom.

Emma sighed when she saw the old-fashioned clawfoot tub. "Wow. It's late, but if it won't disturb anyone downstairs, I'd really like a bath before anything else. There's even bubble bath! Can I use it?"

He laughed. "Go ahead. Then choose any of the bedrooms you want. My mom generally uses the one at the end of the hall, but she won't mind if you want it. And don't worry about breakfast tomorrow. It's practically morning now, and Oliver can wait for your debut."

Leaving her to stare in rapture at the bathtub, Jake strode down the hall to the front staircase and found Oliver pacing in front of the great room fireplace, a frown set firmly in his whisker-stubbled face.

He pulled to a stop when Jake appeared. "I know you and your mom own the lion's share of the ranch, but I'm surprised you didn't let me know you were bringing someone home."

"I didn't know myself, until late last

night. She was still refusing to come here until it was too late to call you."

"She didn't want to come and you still brought her here? Why? I'm guessing it wasn't her wonderful cooking."

"No. But it wasn't anything personal, either. She just needed help, that's all."

"What kind of help? Did she ask for money?"

"There was a man after her, and I know it's true because he confronted both me and a bus driver at a truck stop, asking if we'd seen her."

"So how did she end up with you?"

"She was terrified, obviously. She didn't know me from Adam, but she stowed away in the horse trailer to escape the guy. I discovered she was there when I stopped at a rest stop in western Nebraska."

"So you took her to Denver?"

"If I'd left her behind, who knows what could've happened."

"You couldn't just call the police?"

Jake hesitated. "There are some things

only she should tell you. And no, calling the police wasn't a good option."

Oliver's expression darkened. "So you brought a criminal into this house?"

"No. But there's a chance that she might have been accused of a crime she didn't commit, just so the legal system might find her and haul her back to Chicago. There's a bad element back there that would really like to get their hands on her, Oliver."

"And you believe her?"

"I saw proof."

Oliver's frown softened. "Another wounded bird, then. Just like when you were a boy."

"She's in trouble, yes. But she's sure not a weak little flower begging for protection. Like I said, I had to convince her to come with me. And even then, she said she'd only stay for a short time. The good thing is that a stranger around these parts will really stand out, so if anyone follows her here, we'll know it. I'll have a chance to protect her. And maybe I can end things once and for all, if I just have enough time to make some contacts and follow up before she disappears. If she leaves, who knows how long she'll survive on her own."

"Understood." He bent down in front of the fireplace and stirred the dying embers with a poker. "But she might not be all that safe here, either. We've got trouble, and it's getting worse."

They'd lost five cattle last week, and four the week before…losses that they couldn't afford. Just patrolling and fixing the fence lines was taking all their available time. "You found more fences cut?"

"That, and now we're missing around thirty head of angus from the northwest pasture."

Jared closed his eyes briefly. "You're sure."

"Afraid so. Lane, Ed and I checked. It was the herd that was pregnancy checked last fall and due to calve in another month."

A double loss. Doubly bad for their shaky bottom line. "Did you find tire tracks?"

"Faint, out on Sawmill Road. But with the snow we had last night, they weren't all that clear. Looks like at least a couple of men on horseback and two different semis were up there."

"Did you call the sheriff?"

"You bet. He's already sent out a fax throughout the state to the sheriff's departments, auction houses and vet clinics with a photo of your brand. His secretary is working on the neighboring states."

"All the rustlers have to do is lie low, let those cows calve, then put their own brand on calves. Pretty good timing, don't you think?"

"Bad timing for us."

"Someone knew our herds well enough to know exactly where to look. Any ideas?"

"Only that it must be all connected. The sheriff says there's been no other cattle rustlers reported in this county or any of the neighboring counties for the last three months."

"So someone is targeting us."

"Looks like it. The sheriff wants you to call him. He was asking about any enemies or deals that have gone wrong lately, but I couldn't think of a thing."

"Me neither." Jared let his shoulders slump. "The calves will be lost, no doubt about that. But even the branded mother cows will probably never turn up. With some of the vast ranches in this part of the country, they could stay hidden forever. As long as the ranch does its own basic vet work on them, no one will ever be the wiser."

"You didn't need this on top of everything else. Drought, fuel and feed prices—when is it going to end?"

"I don't know, when there's five hundred cattle out there and only three of us to watch them."

"And Lane, when he's around."

"We shouldn't count on him. He's just a high school kid, and he ought to concentrate on school. Are the broodmares all right?"

"Yep. But they're all up in the smaller pastures near the house now."

"I'm glad you moved them. Let's make sure they stay close by, even if it means we need to hay them all summer. It's a lot more expense, but losing even one of them would be worse."

Oliver rose and put the poker back in its rack. "I'm really sorry about all of this, son. You didn't need more trouble, and that's a fact."

"Anything else?"

"Just the usual. Leah Michaels stopped by, wanting to talk to you about her horse again. I told her you were booked solid with training horses until June, but she never seems to take no for an answer. I think that woman's sweet on you."

"I sure haven't led her on."

Oliver smirked. "And I think she wants you to know she's got money, if you haven't noticed. She must have talked for twenty minutes about the trip she and her daddy are taking to Europe to look for some warmblood mares. If you married her, you could pay off every one of your father's medical bills and be debt-free."

"But I'd be at her father's beck and call, and I'm still not interested."

"Didn't think so. Let's see…the shoer was out Saturday and put bar shoes on the gray gelding. The Masons were here on Saturday to bring in that paint filly for you to start. They want her here sixty days."

"That's already on my schedule."

"And…Ted called." Oliver pursed his lips. "He wanted to talk about the loan we applied for."

Jake had been wandering through the room as they talked, picking up some of the AQHA Champion trophies that now collected dust on most of the flat surfaces in the room. He stopped and turned to face his uncle. "What about?"

"He's not sure he can get the loan approved. If it does go through, it will probably be at a three or four percent higher interest rate."

"That's ridiculous. The first year I got here, we were scrambling to turn this business around. But every year since has been better, and we've never been late on a payment."

"That's what I told him, in case his memory was failing. He said the bank is tightening up its requirements because too many ranchers have defaulted in the last few years. And...you have the ranch equity loan coming due."

"I'll be shipping cattle. They'll have their money on time."

"But," he said, "they don't have it yet. And if you default and they've already approved another loan for us, it would be bad business."

"Bad business, dealing with a family that has dealt with that bank for three generations?"

"His words, not mine."

"How can we expand if we don't bring in new breeding stock? That Breeder's Select angus sale is in just six months. I'll go talk to him tomorrow."

"I'll come, too. Though the temptation to toss him out the window might be too great to bear. That arrogance of his is what drives me up the wall."

Jake laughed. "Maybe I'd be safer leaving you home."

"Nahh. I'll be on my best behavior." Oliver clapped Jake on the shoulder. "We'll get through this, just like your dad did when he had some tough times through the years."

A heavy weight of guilt settled over Jake's shoulders. "I just wish I'd known how things were going around here."

"It wasn't your fault, son. He was proud of your career, and was adamant about letting you follow your heart. He didn't want any of us to know how sick he really was...or how much it drove him into debt. I was even living here, and I didn't know he was that bad until just months before he died."

She was cold. So very cold. Awakening with a start, Emma sat upright, splashing cold water everywhere. The fragrant strawberry bubbles were long gone; the hot, steamy, wonderful bath water had turned frigid.

Shaking, she stepped over the high sides of the tub and wrapped a pink towel around her hair, then used a second one to vigorously dry herself off. She glanced at her wristwatch on the edge of the sink. How could it be six in the morning already?

And how could she have fallen asleep in the tub, and missed the chance for a wonderful night in one of those lovely four-poster beds piled with down comforters?

Instead of putting on her nightgown, she padded glumly back to the corner bedroom facing the barns. "At least Oliver can have his breakfast made for him after all," she muttered to herself as she pulled on jeans and a sweatshirt from the shopping bags she'd dropped on the floor. He hadn't seemed very pleased to see her.

She dragged a hairbrush through her hair, which was already springing up into wild curls, and gathered the towels to hang in the bathroom.

She blinked and stared in horror at the smears of cheap auburn hair color that had ruined one of the towels, then turned to look at herself in the mirror above the oak dresser.

Much of the hair color had washed away, leaving her light blond hair colored in cammo-mottled shades from pale pink to red. Groaning, she hurried back to the bathroom, grabbed the shampoo and washed her hair again in the sink, with the hottest water she could bear, sudsing and rinsing three times before giving herself a wary look in the mirror.

It was wet and dark, but surely it was better. Wasn't it? She towel dried it again, fluffed it with her fingertips and quietly slipped down the back stairs to the kitchen.

The room was dark and peaceful, save for a dim light left on over the sink. Only the steady hum of the refrigerator and the quiet tick-tick-tick of the clock over the stove broke the silence, except for the occasional whinny of a horse somewhere outside.

The refrigerator was sparsely stocked, though she did find a pound of bacon, a carton of eggs, milk and butter, along with a collection of condiments. The bottom drawer held potatoes—*who* would store potatoes in the fridge?—plus oranges and apples.

Rescuing the potatoes from the cold

temperature, she also pulled out some oranges and then starting searching for the cookware.

At the sound of bare feet padding across the oak wood floor, she spun around, feeling as if she'd been caught with her hands in a cookie jar and found herself face-to-face with a teenage boy who had just come around the corner.

His eyes widened with shock and a touch of fear. "Who are you—and what are you taking?" He spun around. "Dad! Dad—there's someone in the house stealing stuff."

"Hush." She reached out to catch his fall as he floundered backward, but his arm slipped through her grasp and he caught his elbow against the edge of the counter.

He wavered there, caught between running and making a stand against a dangerous intruder, and she tried to hide her smile at his awkward teenage bravado. "I'm Emma. I came with Jake late last night, and we woke up your dad, so he's probably sleeping. You must be Lane. Right?"

"Nobody said anything about you coming," he retorted, rubbing his elbow. His belligerent gaze veered up to her hair and stayed there. "What are you, some kind of druggie gypsy or something?"

She hid a smile. "Actually, I'm a librarian."

"Yeah, right. Just like every librarian *I* ever saw." He looked over his shoulder and yelled around the corner for his dad again at the top of his lungs.

"It's truc. But right now, I'm on sort of a…a sabbatical. That's when someone takes time off to do something different. I decided it might be fun to work here for a while as a cook and a housekeeper." She held up the carton of eggs. "How do you like them, scrambled? Fried?"

His eyebrows drew together. "You're here to be a cook?"

"That's right. So if you could help me

find the electric fry pan and a regular skillet, I could make your breakfast."

When he didn't move, she shrugged and started hunting for the equipment she needed. "Here we go."

She lugged a heavy cast-iron fry pan onto the stove, then retrieved an electric skillet from the corner carousel cupboard and set it on the counter.

"You really are gonna be the cook, and Dad isn't gonna do it anymore?" The note of hope in his voice was unmistakable.

"I will be for a while," she said carefully. "Not forever. But if you three guys don't like my cooking, or I decide this job just isn't right for me, then I'll pack up and go. Fair enough?"

"Wow." His gaze zeroed in on her hair again. "Is that, like, your real hair?"

"Real hair, wrong color. I hope it washes out in a few days. So what will it be? From what I've found around here, I can make most any kind of eggs, plus bacon and toast, or I could do pancakes."

"Everything, except the toast. Scrambled eggs with cheddar cheese."

"Works for me." She pulled a box of pancake mix out of the cupboard and stirred up a batch, then started the bacon frying. "Have you lived here all your life?"

"Nah." A note of loneliness crept into his voice. "We moved here when I was ten. Dad lost his job at the feed store, so he came to work for Uncle Ray and Mom did all the cooking. But she died a year ago. Right on Valentine's Day."

"I'm sorry to hear that. My mom died last year. It's awfully tough, isn't it?"

He nodded, his eyes suspiciously bright. "Now it's just Dad and me. And Jake. He's my cousin, but he's waaay older."

"Old as the hills?" she teased.

"Over thirty, at least."

The back door opened on a gust of snow-laden wind and both Jake and Oliver stepped inside the entryway, stamped the snow from their boots and started peeling off layers of coats and clothes.

"Hey, Jake," Lane called out. "How old are you? She wants to know."

"No. I don't. I mean, Lane was just talking, a-and—" Flustered and embarrassed at the way both men were regarding her, she stammered to a halt. "Forget it."

Jake eyed her with amusement. "Thirty-two. Interesting hair, by the way. I think I like it better pink."

"It won't be nearly as interesting later. I promise." She started cracking the eggs into a bowl. "Lane wants scrambled eggs and cheese with his pancakes and bacon. How about you two?"

Jake moved to the sink and started making a pot of coffee. "Sounds good to me."

Oliver grunted his assent as he grabbed an orange and settled down at the round oak table by the windows. He methodically peeled it, then began breaking it apart. He paused and looked at her over the segments. "So where is it you came from?"

"Chicago, most recently."

"And where is it you hope to end up? When you leave here, that is."

"*Dad,*" Lane stage-whispered, his embarrassment obvious in the bright spots of color on his cheekbones.

"I'm just asking. Can't I do that?"

"I'd like to live somewhere in the Rockies, where I can find a job and an affordable place to live." She smiled gently at Oliver, understanding that there was real concern under his bluster.

After spraying the cast-iron skillet with pan release, she dropped in a couple tablespoons of butter, waited for it to sizzle, then poured in the eggs. She poured the pancake batter into the other pan and flipped over the sizzling bacon slices.

"I told Jake I could stay here for a little while, but I've got places to go if this arrangement doesn't work out for everyone. I understand your concern about a complete stranger moving into the house, Oliver. I'd be worried, too, if I had a child to think about. I won't mind a bit if I need to move on."

"Well, I will." Jake leveled a look at Oliver, then flipped the coffeemaker switch and turned to lean against the counter. "Because the longer Emma sticks around, the safer—" His gaze skated over to Lane, and he reframed his words. "The better it will be for all of us. We've all missed Aunt Francis a lot, and it will be nice to have a woman's cooking again. Right?"

Oliver grunted.

"If I was as rude as you, I'd be grounded," Lane grumbled, glaring at his dad. "Big-time."

"Lane." The warning note in Oliver's voice was unmistakable.

"It's true." The teenager stalked out of the kitchen and down the hall. A moment later, his bedroom door slammed.

"I'm sorry," Emma said quietly. "I didn't mean to start anything between you two."

She found maple syrup in the refrigerator, heated it in the microwave, set the table and brought over heaping plates to Oliver and Jake.

"Snow's coming so we won't be making it to church this morning," Oliver said gruffly. "Might as well get yourself a plate and join us."

"In a minute." She finished plating up breakfast for Lane and put it on a tray with a glass of milk, and took it to his room.

"Go away," he muttered when she knocked on his door.

"It's me, Emma. I have your breakfast here." When he didn't answer, she added, "And this tray is getting really heavy. Please open the door."

She heard him shuffle to the door, and he pulled it open. "Here you go, I just didn't want your food to get cold."

He mumbled thanks as he took the tray from her, and then he looked up, his eyes wide. "You did this for me?"

"Just for you. Chocolate chip pancakes were always my favorite."

"I haven't had these since my m-mom died." His voice wobbled, and the tips of his ears turned pink. He ducked his head. "Thanks."

"You're welcome, Lane. And don't be too upset with your dad. He's only being cautious, and in his shoes, I would be, too. I don't blame him a bit."

But instead of going back to the kitchen, she headed quietly upstairs to stand at her bedroom window.

They were on a hill, she realized. On a good day one could probably see for miles. But snow flurries were dancing in giddy swirls past her window and the terrain was an endless sea of snow, blending sky and horizon into an unbroken wall of white. The vast panorama of nothingness seemed strangely confining, because she could see no signs of other ranches, no roads that could take her to someplace else.

And now she had no car of her own, and was trapped in an isolated place with a surly teenager, plus one man who had disliked her on sight, and another who now knew exactly how much of a liability she was and probably wished he'd left her in Denver.

ELEVEN

Though Jake told Emma it was Sunday and she could start working around the place tomorrow, she bustled through the main floor of the house all day, dusting and polishing furniture, vacuuming and washing the window panes on the inside.

By five o'clock, even Oliver had told her to stop working so hard, but then she got busy on supper, and soon the aroma wafting from the kitchen smelled so good that Jake had been back four times to ask her what she was making.

"Something easy and good. I hope." She bit her lip and peered at the screen of the minilaptop she'd pulled out of her purse and placed on the kitchen counter. "If it isn't, then I'll really wonder about all of those five star ratings it got on this website."

Jake thought about Oliver's meat-and-potatoes rancher's tastes. "This isn't going to be too exotic, is it?"

"Don't worry," she said drily. "I can only work with what you have here, so you won't be finding any escargot or calamari on your plate. But if I'm going to do much cooking while I'm here, I've got to write up a list and get to a grocery store before long."

"Make the list and I'll go into town tomorrow morning. There's a chance of heavy snow predicted for tomorrow night, and after that it might be a while before we can get out."

"The roads should be okay by the end of the week, though. Right?"

"As far as the snow, that's hard to say. More snow is predicted for Wednesday and Thursday, and even after we clear our own roads there's still over twenty miles of county highway to town."

"Doesn't the county take care of it?"

"Eventually, but we're usually last on the list for the county plows. The Rocking K is the only ranch this far out on County 73, and the road dead-ends at the edge of the state forest."

"There's only one way to town?"

"There's a network of low-maintenance roads through the foothills in this area, but they would take twice as long and they're only plowed now and then."

Her face fell. "So we could be snow-bound."

"Not necessarily. The weather pattern could veer off and dump snow on someone else, in which case Lane will be really disappointed." Jake laughed. "Not that I blame him. I used to love school cancellations, too."

She shivered. "But what if you need help...or really have to leave?"

"Don't worry about it. We just prepare for the worst and hope for the best out here, weatherwise. As long as we don't lose our electricity, it's fine. Even then, we always manage."

Lane ambled into the room and snagged a Pepsi out of the refrigerator. "But chores are about ten times harder," he grumbled as he pried off the pop-top. "Just try and keep the water tanks open when it's twenty below and the electric tank heaters aren't working."

He sauntered back down the hall to his room.

"Teenagers," Jake said with a dry laugh. "He makes it sound like we have him out there with an ice pick. We just switch to old-fashioned stock tank heaters that burn oil if the electricity goes out."

Emma fidgeted with a dish towel. "If you go to town, I want to come, too."

"You'll be safer here."

"On an isolated ranch with one dependable access road? Where would I run to if something bad happened? I'm better off with options."

"But Oliver and Lane are here, as well as the dogs."

"Don't leave me behind, Jake. Please."

The worry in her pretty hazel eyes was unmistakable, and he realized just how much he was coming to care for her. After all his resolutions about avoiding emotional entanglements after Maura left, what had he gotten himself into?

"You wanna come outside with me and see my horse?" Lane had sat in stubborn silence during supper, refusing to look up at his father despite several conversational gambits.

Now, with Oliver and Jake conferring back in Jake's office, Lane had draped himself over the breakfast bar in the kitchen with iPod earbuds in his ears and a bored expression on his face. His fingers tapped to the rhythm of music only he could hear.

Emma sprinkled two cups of sharp cheddar over the breakfast casserole for tomorrow, covered the pan with plastic wrap and slid it into the refrigerator. "I'd like that."

"Do you ride?"

"Just a pony when I was little." She moved to the sink to wash and dry her hands. "After that, I only rode at scout camp. I always dreamed of having a horse, but never could because...well, we moved a lot."

"You could ride mine if you want."

"I'd like that someday. Maybe when it's not so cold." She caught her words too late. By then she'd be long gone to who knew where. "It would be fun to see you ride, though."

"How about now? You need boots if you're going to the barn, though. Jake's orders." He unfolded himself and stretched, all long limbs and bony angles, then padded in his stocking feet to the coat closet at the back door. He sorted through the closet and withdrew a pair that looked like silver ostrich leather. "These might fit."

"You're sure it's okay? They look awfully nice."

He snickered as he studied the ornate butterfly cutwork exposing a layer of hot pink leather. "They look pretty silly if you ask me. But so is the person who used to wear them around here. Go figure."

Emma hesitated. "Jake's sister?"

"*She's* cool." He rolled his eyes. "Try Maura."

"And she is…"

"The crazy lady who divorced Jake for some rich dude with a potbelly."

"He was *married?*"

"Not for long, and it was a bad deal. She left a bunch of stuff here, and when she said she didn't want it, Jake and my dad finally threw most of it out. They kept some of the boots for when customers fly in and want to ride their horses."

Emma gingerly tugged on the boots, and

then Lane handed her a heavy down jacket and gloves emanating a strong aroma of horse. "You can always grab anything on the hooks, except Dad's brown jacket and Jake's black one."

She followed him out into the night. Glittery snow crunched under their feet as they walked across the yard, out the gate and then across the broad parking area to the main horse barn. The snow on either side of the cleared path was up to her knees.

"The sky is amazing out here," she called out, laughing when her boot skidded and she had to flail her arms to stay upright. "Have you ever heard of light pollution?"

"Light what?"

"It's what we have back in Chicago and all of the big cities. When millions of artificial lights are lit up at night the glow makes it hard to see many stars. But out here, wow! I can't believe how many stars you can see. It's like someone threw a bowl of sugar across the sky."

At the horse barn, Lane led her through a door leading into a tack room and turned on the light. The room inside was pine-paneled, neatly swept, with a wall of five-tiered saddle racks and rows of horizontal racks holding silver-mounted halters and bridles.

A big picture window dominated the op-posite wall, reflecting their images as they headed across the room. Cats of all colors appeared from their cozy nests on the tops of stacked blankets.

Two calicos and a tabby wound around her ankles until she finally gave up and stopped to pet them. "So do these sweeties have names?"

"Some do." Lane flipped a row of wall switches and the dark cave beyond the window lit up, revealing an indoor arena. "If you want to stay in here where it's warm, I can go get my horse and turn him out. Fred always bucks like mad when he goes out there. It's fun to watch."

"Fred?"

"His real name is Tucker's Pine Bar because of his bloodlines. Fred fits him better."

"I'd like to follow you around and see the barn, if that's okay. I think this tack room is nicer than some people's houses."

"Jake and Dad worked really hard on this place after Uncle Ray died, because Jake started training and it had to be nice for customers."

The aisle was broad and similar to the sale barn she'd been in, but here the stall fronts were paneled in burnished oak that had been constructed with exquisite attention to detail. Gleaming horses, each clad in a heavy horse blanket, came to the bars of their stalls and nickered.

"One thing I forgot to—"

A cacophony of squawks and honks, rapid as machine-gun fire, erupted from within a stall to her left. A second later an explosion of white feathers and wide, flapping wings flew out of the open door. The long, cobralike neck snaked out well in front of a giant bird's body.

It beat its wings harder to gain some lift off, its open beak headed straight for her face. She stumbled backward with her hands in front of her.

"Gilbert!" Lane stepped between her and the furious bird and somehow managed a good enough hold on the flapping, squirming bird to pull it away, its wings flapping furiously and webbed feet pedaling. The nonstop litany of honks and squawks advertised its fury in no uncertain terms.

Lane staggered, then somehow managed to wrestle it back into the open stall and shut the door.

She struggled to catch her breath, her pulse pounding, and then broke into helpless laughter. "You know, Jake said something about a goose being good protection. I thought he was joking."

"I would never joke about that." Jake came through the tack room door and shut it behind him. "He's so territorial that sometimes he puts on his big show when I come into the barn, and I'm even the one who feeds him."

"And getting bit by a big, stupid goose is not fun," Lane grumbled, dusting feathers off his jacket.

Jake grinned. "The good thing is that he helps desensitize the horses to unexpected commotions."

"And the bad thing is that he *causes* all those unexpected commotions. One day he spooked my horse and I got dumped, then he ran over and bit my ear. But he *really* hated Maura," Lane added with obvious relish. "He went after her on sight."

"Anything else I should know about out here?"

Lane shrugged. "The dogs are all fine once they know you. But be careful if you came out here at night. Jake arms the security system at eleven."

"Security?" Astonished, she turned away from the horse she was petting through the bars to look at him. "I thought we were in the middle of nowhere."

"There's a lot of expensive horseflesh in here, not to mention the show equipment. I'd just rather play it safe."

Apparently a consistent theme in his life, from belligerent birds to stowaways he found hiding in his horse trailer.

Lane led Fred, his burly-looking gray horse, out of its stall and down the aisle. "If you want to see him play, we should go back into the tack room, Emma," he called out over his shoulder.

She smiled. "I think I'd better. He seems pretty proud of that horse."

"I think you've made a friend. Lane doesn't take this well to everyone."

"I'm sure it was just the chocolate chip pancakes. And maybe, the chance to talk to someone with pink hair. That doesn't happen every day out here, I'm sure."

Jake chuckled as he turned and opened

the tack room door, and ushered her inside.

Emma went to stand at the window and watched Lane unsnap the lead rope on Fred's halter. The gelding trotted a few steps. Its knees buckled and it dropped to the ground to roll, then it awkwardly regained its feet and burst into a round of wild bucking before racing in ever widening circles.

Jake came to stand beside her. "I need to ask you a few questions."

"Fire away."

"Don't take this wrong, but did you ever wonder about the circumstances when you and your family saw the senator being murdered?"

She angled a glance at him, and shook her head. "Why would I? It was an awful coincidence, nothing more."

"But why were you there, at just that moment?"

His question unleashed a landslide of memories. Two hard-eyed investigators had questioned her alone, in a cold, gray and frightening room somewhere in the police station. They'd grilled her, picking at every word she said, until she'd started to cry, and then the male investigator had sworn under his breath and stalked away.

Testifying in court had been even worse.

She felt herself bristle. "Why are you asking? We were victims, too, remember? We tried to do the right thing and ended up paying for it ever since."

"I understand. I know you loved your dad and that you lost him a short time ago. But that was a mighty big coincidence, being in that nearly empty parking garage, at that particular moment."

"We got *lost,* Jake. Dad was really angry, circling city blocks. He said he was trying to find the right parking ramp for our hotel. I think maybe all of the one-way streets made it more frustrating, or something. But that's all I remember. I was only nine. I was sitting in the backseat, reading a book. I didn't pay any attention until we were in the garage."

"And what did you see?"

She huffed out an impatient breath. "What I told everyone, too many times to count. Exactly what I said in court."

"Just humor me."

She closed her eyes, and suddenly she was back in that hot, airless courtroom during the first trial with everyone staring at her, while a lawyer smirked and tried to make everyone think she was a liar.

She'd worn a pink dress, and she could still feel the hard wooden chair in the witness box, slick with nervous perspiration from her bare thighs.

The hard, cold glare of the defendant had terrified her.

"There were three men," she recited. "Two had guns. The tallest one with silver hair was wearing a suit, and he was backing away from the others with his hands in front of him. He was pleading with them, though I couldn't hear all the words. The other two men were shouting, too—and then they shot him. Dad swore, like he was really angry. Then he stomped on the accelerator and drove like crazy out of the parking ramp. The car tires squealed on the tight corners and I was sure we were going to have a wreck. But he managed to drive away."

"What then?"

"Dad said not to say anything about it. He said he would take care of everything."

"Did he?"

"He later testified that he didn't want to get involved, because those men looked dangerous and he was afraid for our safety. But our rental car was picked up on a parking ramp surveillance camera, so the investigators tracked us down."

"Did you ever see him acting suspicious? Secretive?"

"No. Yes—I don't know. He went to work, came home. I went to school, came home. It always seemed like a routine, ordinary life to me."

"The thing that keeps bothering me is the timetable. Rodriguez had no need to wait fourteen years to pay you and your family back after your testimony helped put him on death row. He had the power and money to put out a contract on all of you at any time. If I were in his shoes, I'd be livid, and I'd make sure the punishment was swift and fatal."

"This is nothing new to me. So, where is this leading?"

"What if your dad wasn't such an innocent bystander after all?"

She stiffened. "That's *impossible*."

"Is it? What if he was involved with that cartel at, say, just a business level. Maybe he'd even been coerced, then found himself bound because of threats against his family. He might have known the location of a *lot* of money, or of something terribly valuable. Not buried under some rock, but stashed in offshore accounts somewhere. Rodriguez might not trust an underling to go after and transport something of such immense value, which might account for the reason he waited for his most trusted associates to get out of prison."

"But Dad wasn't like that. He was a good man. Honest and kind. And he liked to laugh." Her eyebrows drew together. "At least he did when I was small."

"Do you remember what he did for a living when you were young?"

"This is ridiculous. I can't believe that you're trying to make him into something he wasn't. We saw a murder. We testified. End of story."

"Okay, but the murder took place a year after your adoption. What did he do for a living then?"

She paced around the tack room, then came back again, clearly agitated. "He always wore a suit. He went to an office."

"Did you ever see his office?"

"Once, maybe twice. It was pretty boring for a child my age."

"I talked to one of my old contacts—a P.I. in Wyoming, and asked him to do a little checking. Did you know that your dad worked at an accounting firm at the time of your adoption, but was fired shortly afterward?"

"No."

"At the time, the standard terms at the adoption agency stated that either the adoption service or the adoptive family could back out of their agreement within six months after a child was placed, believe it or not. Being suddenly jobless wouldn't have been viewed favorably. Maybe that alone could've been enough motivation to drive your father to do something desperate...something he normally wouldn't even consider. Can you imagine facing the threat of losing a child that you'd longed for, and now loved with all your heart?"

She stared at Jake with obvious disbelief. "You think my dad got involved with a *drug* cartel? An ordinary, middle-class family man? That's ridiculous."

"Not if he was desperate enough and

they courted him for his accounting and business skills. If they gave him a good salary, careful distance from the less reputable sides of the business, everything might have appeared perfectly normal on the surface."

She fell silent, her eyes troubled.

"Then I started to wonder...what hornet's nest could he stir up later—and why—especially since he'd been able to live in peaceful obscurity with WITSEC for so long?"

"My mom's death hit him really hard. He was so angry, so bitter. He wouldn't talk to me about it."

"You'll probably never know if her death was truly an accident, or if it was caused by those guys from the past. But maybe your dad thought his old enemies had discovered your identities and location, and feared that you could be next. So he tried to barter for your safety with important information he still had...only he got killed instead."

"This is making my head spin."

"But it starts to make sense, once you study it awhile. Ask yourself why there are people after you. People who have had any number of chances to take you out. But they don't want you dead, they want you *alive*. Why? I started researching that cartel on the internet, and found some pretty interesting stuff. Maybe these guys think you hold the keys to a tremendous cache of funds—possibly in gold or diamonds—that's supposedly part of the Rodriguez hidden fortune."

"That's crazy."

"Maybe not. They might think your dad told you everything, so you'd have that bargaining chip, as well. These people are dead serious if they're trying to track you across the country. The longer you lay low here, the more time I've got to figure out exactly who they are."

"I appreciate that. Honestly, I do. But how could you find answers from way out here?"

"Give me the internet and my smart phone, and I've got an instant office anywhere—access to the world. It's unbelievable what kind of information an investigator can glean from the internet. I've also called in some old favors, and now I'm waiting to hear back."

"Favors? Sounds a little like the Mafia."

"Nope. Just more people I knew during my law enforcement days. And it's like a network—they all have connections, too, and some of them could be useful."

"Maybe it would be better if I just disappeared. I did have a good plan in place, Jake."

"You could. But it hasn't exactly gone well so far, and what if the next step doesn't work so well, either? Imagine what lengths these people would go to if they caught you and tried to force you to give the location of Rodriguez's fortune?"

She paled. "I don't know anything."

"But they wouldn't believe you, and they certainly wouldn't let you go once you could identify them. That's why I'm hoping you'll stay around, Emma. The only way for you to have a life again is if we can take these guys down. And that's what I plan to do."

TWELVE

When Jake first told her that False Lake had a couple thousand inhabitants, she hadn't clearly envisioned just how small a town that size would be...or how charming.

Set against a backdrop of the towering Rockies, Main Street offered a four-block-long commercial area straight out of the Old West, with tall, old-fashioned storefronts and wooden sidewalks running along the businesses on either side of the street.

Where many small towns seemed to have a lot of buildings for rent and a sad air of commercial doom, this one appeared vibrant, with outfitters, bait and tackle shops, bike shops, gifts and sundries predominating, clearly appealing to the tourist trade. On the edge of town, there were clusters of rental cabins and several charming bed-and-breakfasts, though only one appeared to be open during the off-season.

Jake parked in front of the grocery. "I'm going across the street to the vet clinic and pick up some amoxicillin. I'll be back over to pay for everything, okay? Then we'll run to the post office and have those packages forwarded from Deer Lodge."

Emma nodded and pulled her cap low over her head to cover up her pink hair, then retrieved the grocery list out of her jacket pocket. "No problem."

The aisles were crowded, so apparently other people were expecting bad weather, too.

A lovely redhead coming from the opposite direction in the dairy aisle stopped and touched Emma's arm as she passed. "Looks like a bad one coming, doesn't it?"

Startled at the random and unexpected greeting, Emma darted a quick look at her face but found only open friendliness there. "Um…yes."

"It's lucky Jake made it back when he did, or he might've had to cool his heels in town for a few days." The woman laughed. "I'm sorry, I saw you two drive in a minute ago. I'm Betsy, Pastor Will Anderson's wife. From your expression, I'll bet you're from a big city. When I first moved here, I was surprised every time someone stopped to chat, since I didn't know a soul."

"I'm Emma. I'll be working out at his ranch for a while. Just on a trial basis so far."

"Well, welcome to False Lake. I hope you'll feel welcome to come to church with the Kincaids next Sunday." Betsy winked. "We are in *desperate* need for more people in the choir."

"Thanks." Accustomed to the complete anonymity of living in an urban area where no one knew her name, Betsy's friendliness surprised and delighted her... but she felt a tinge of sadness, as well.

Cradled in the shadows of the soaring Rockies, False Lake was a quaint and charming little town. The scenery in every direction was breathtaking. But she was going to be here only a short time and there'd be no point in becoming too comfortable because nothing in her life was permanent. Eighteen years in the WITSEC program had taught her that.

Emma hurried through the store, picking up everything on her shopping list. She bumped into Betsy in nearly every aisle and they both laughed, but Emma kept moving.

At the front of the store she waited near the cash register line. She drummed her fingers on the cart handle, waiting for Jake to appear and fielding the welcomes and curiosity of four other locals who apparently had seen her drive down Main Street in Jake's truck, too.

She was beginning to realize that he'd been exactly right about this town. A stranger wouldn't pass by unnoticed, especially in the off-season months when tourists weren't flocking to the Rockies.

Through the front window she saw him saunter across the street with a stunning blonde at his side. She wore a waist-hugging red leather jacket, black slacks and knee-high leather boots, and a swath of silky hair swung at her shoulders. Her outfit probably cost more than Emma had earned in a month at the library, and even at a distance, she could see that the woman was gorgeous.

Jake had implied that he had no romantic entanglements, but from the way the woman was hanging on his arm, that didn't seem to be the case at all. *Men.*

Not that Emma cared.

The two of them came into the store and she suddenly felt every bit the country mouse in the presence of a princess as the woman zeroed in on her and strode forward.

"Well, well," she gushed, glancing prettily over her shoulder at Jake. "You didn't tell me she was such a cute little thing."

Jake gave her a stony look.

"I'm Maura." The woman swooped in and gave Emma a sharp head to toe glance, her expression far less friendly than the tone of her voice. "I'm so glad to hear the guys finally found someone to keep up that place."

This was Maura of the silver-and-pink cowboy boots, apparently. "Just a trial basis."

"Well, I'm sure they'll all appreciate the help. I worry about them, not having decent meals." Maura rested a possessive hand on Jake's arm. "But if it doesn't work out for all of you, I imagine this might be a good time to apply for seasonal housekeeping jobs at the little motels and cabin resorts around here. The tourist traffic picks up in early June."

With a farewell flutter of her long mauve fingernails, she left the store.

"Are you ready to check out?"

Jake's grim smile lacked any warmth at all...probably because he was now wondering why he was bothering with a woman like Emma at all. Had he really been married to such a gorgeous creature?

She nodded and shoved her cart to the register and loaded the groceries onto the conveyor belt, then moved ahead to stare out the front window while Jake settled up.

She'd always known her time with him would be very limited. Yet, despite her firm resolutions, she'd been more drawn to him with each passing day. Just a single sidelong glance from him had the power to make her insides flutter. An inadvertent touch made her skin tingle and her heart stumble.

But far more than that physical attraction, he was a protector. An intriguing man with determination and honor, and a strong sense of right and wrong. The kind of man who would take in a stray like her and refuse to back away from trouble.

The kind of guy she'd dreamed of, believing that he would only exist between the pages of a good book or as a hero in some movie.

But even if her troubles were to disappear tomorrow, the past few minutes had reminded her of one very important fact.

There would never be any point in staying here, because Jake Kincaid was out of her league.

After stowing the groceries in the backseat of the truck, Jake drove down to the post office so Emma could discuss the forwarding of her packages from Deer Lodge to False Lake. Already there was a damp, heavy feel to the air, and an ominous east wind was picking up, making her feel edgy and watchful of the leaden sky. An inner voice urged her to pack up and flee. But surely it was just a primitive response to the falling barometric pressure prior to a storm that made even animals edgy. Wasn't it?

"Feels like snow," Jake said as they waited for Doris, the portly silver-haired postmistress, to finish with the customer ahead of them.

Emma nodded, glancing over her shoulder for the third time since they'd arrived. Her edginess grew. Maybe she should have listened and stayed at the ranch.

No one had followed them here, she was sure of it. They'd been practically the only ones on the highway during the long drive through the night. But tracing a truck license plate wouldn't be that hard for someone who knew how...

"You're awfully quiet. I don't suppose it was Maura. She can be a little...overpowering at times."

"No. Of course not."

She fidgeted with the scarf she'd knotted

around her neck. "I just want to get this done so we can be on our way."

"I've got one more stop to make at the bank, but it shouldn't take long. You can come in and wait in the lobby if you want. But there's a little bookstore next to it, and our church runs a consignment store on the other side if you want something to do."

The elderly woman in front of them moved on, and Emma stepped forward to explain her request to Doris. She retrieved a receipt from her purse. "Here's the tracking number."

"And I can vouch for her," Jake drawled.

"Jake was in my Sunday school class in third grade, and he was quite a rascal." Doris's faded blue eyes twinkled. "Let me make a quick call to see if those packages have even arrived up there, so you'll have an idea about when to come back into town to get them."

She bustled away and returned a few minutes later. This time, she regarded

Emma with an air of doubt. "I know you have a slip showing you sent them, but those packages aren't there."

Emma paled. "That can't be."

Doris shrugged. "I asked twice. Could be delayed because of the blizzard that went through Nebraska and Colorado. And, one of the USPS semis was involved in a six-vehicle pileup, though I'm sure all of the mail was recovered. I did explain the situation and ask them to forward your packages here when they do show up, so check back again in a few days."

Sending them ahead had seemed like a good idea at the time. After losing her luggage back in Ogallala, she'd been sure of it. But now everything she needed for her new future was lost and she couldn't leave here until it turned up.

Jake curved an arm around her shoulders and gave her a quick hug. "It isn't the end of the world, Emma. Your things will show up."

She dredged up a smile. "You're right. Not a big deal."

But a feeling of dread had been building inside her since she'd first awakened this morning, and the persistent feeling would not go away.

Even now, with Jake at her side as they went out to the truck, she had an uneasy sense that someone was in every shadow along Main Street, watching her. Waiting for the right moment to make a move.

Was it just her overactive imagination, or had trouble really followed her here?

"Good to see you, buddy." Ted Barnes pumped Jake's hand and clapped him on the shoulder, then closed his office door behind them. He waved Jake toward one of the leather chairs in front of his oversize mahogany desk. "What can I do for you today?"

He was as superficial and effusive as ever, and his slightly supercilious smirk was already in place, reminiscent of the

boy he'd been in high school. It was probably a good thing Oliver had decided to
stay home and watch over a mare getting
ready to foal.

"Oliver and I talked to you earlier this
year about a loan designated for building
up our angus breeding program. There's a
big Breeders Select sale coming up in less
than six weeks that is offering the bloodlines we need. But Oliver tells me that you
aren't sure you can approve it."

Ted folded his hands on the gleaming
surface of his desk. "It's not just up to me,
of course."

"It has been in the past."

"Not so. Everything has to be approved,
but in the past, the economy was better so
it was a swift, easy process. We had overly
optimistic trust in our friends, however.
In the last couple years, far too many of
them have defaulted, and then the bank
has had to deal with taking over ranches,
cars…you name it."

"My grandfather banked here. In all the

years our family has done business with this bank we've never had any issues."

Ted bared his teeth in a semblance of a smile. "But you're at the helm now, Jake. An unknown entity. And you've got a whopper of a ranch equity loan coming due in three weeks based on...I believe... your father's last medical bills."

"I'm hauling cattle to a sale the weekend before, and I've got a couple of top geldings that will be going to a reining futurity sale. There will be no problem paying it off."

"When you do pay off that loan on time, come back in and we'll talk. I can't guarantee the interest rate will be as favorable as it was when we first talked about this, though."

"There's less than two weeks between the time I can pay off that equity loan and the day I need to leave for the angus sale. Given your paperwork and all, what are the chances that I'll have the new loan approved in time?"

Ted had been a nerdy kid in high school, one who buttered up teachers and was a little too proud of his scholastic achievements. He'd been disliked by a lot of kids. But now he had power, and he clearly relished it. He studied his fingernails. "Fair."

Reining in his frustration, Jake stood. "Then maybe I need to find a different bank."

"You could. Yes, of course you could… but of course they'll check every last detail of your financial history. If you can find one that isn't a little leery about your situation with that large loan coming due—or can set up a new loan at a better rate, go for it. But we're local and we'll do our best."

THIRTEEN

Jake stared out the window of his office at the gusts of snow blowing past, then turned back to his computer monitor and continued scrolling through all of the email that had come through in the past twelve hours.

Since arriving home from Denver he'd spent his spare moments searching the internet for details of the Rodriguez case, and for any information he could find on the trial itself.

The drug lord was in federal prison without any chance of parole, convicted of drug trafficking and two cases of murder-for-hire, so he'd never again see the light of day as a free man. Jake had found the names of his team of lawyers and had contacted them through their law office website, to no avail. He'd called the office twice, but hadn't gotten past the secretary.

Once again, he looked at the number he'd scribbled on a notepad and touched the numbers on the screen of his phone. After a dozen rings, he'd started to end the call when a surly male voice came on the line.

"Yes?"

"I'd like to talk to John Burton or Frank Carlton."

"Yeah, well…the secretary takes care of these things and she's gone. Call back."

"Please—I've been trying for days, and no one has returned my calls. I'm…involved in a case in Montana, and I need to talk to someone about Eduardo Rodriguez."

A stony silence lengthened before the man cleared his throat. "Why?" His voice was filled with suspicion. "Are you some sort of reporter?"

"No."

"Rodriguez isn't interested in any book deals."

"It's not that, either. It's a little complicated, but I'm investigating a series of crimes against some witnesses in the trial. I need information."

"He's on death row. He's had a conversion of faith. He's not interested in revenge, if that's what you're thinking. He's trying to straighten out his life, with whatever time he has left."

"And you believe it?"

"Why wouldn't I? No matter what he says or does or claims to think, he's got multiple federal sentences and he will either die on death row of his bladder cancer or he'll die by injection. There's no point in lying at this point. It would gain him nothing. He says he's trying to make amends and is praying for forgiveness, and yes, I do believe him."

"What about visitors? Would he agree to see me?"

"You'd come clear from Montana? Believe me, there's no point. He's got a short list of who he has agreed to see, and it's just family and us."

"But to resolve an old case…"

"Join the club. With his past, there's a line clear to Kalamazoo of people who would like just five minutes with him to ask about the death of someone they knew, or a crime they were charged with that might have been done by one of his men. All pure speculation and false hopes, of course."

"How often does he ask to see his lawyers?"

"He talks to John maybe once a month. Not about appeals, just…talk."

"Can you at least pass a question along for me?"

The man made an impatient sound in his throat.

"It involves a witness in the trial. Just

in the last year, two members of a family were murdered and now someone is after the daughter. It's too much of a coincidence to imagine that there isn't some sort of connection to that trial. This was just an ordinary, law-abiding family, and now she is terrified."

"And this happened fourteen years after the trial."

"I don't understand that, either, but I'm just trying to cover all the bases to keep her safe. Maybe Rodriguez wouldn't give a straight answer anyway, but I thought if I could just talk to him face-to-face, maybe he'd relent. I know he has children of his own."

"Give me your email address and phone number. I'll see what we can do—no promises, understand?"

"Understood. And you are…"

"Frank," he finally added in a grudging tone after a long silence. "But as the old saying goes, don't call us, we'll call you.

If we get any information you can use. But honestly, don't hold your breath."

Ever since they'd come back from town this morning, the snow had grown heavier and the wind had started to howl. Just the sound of it made Emma feel cold as she finished mopping the kitchen floor.

A five-pound beef roast, potatoes, carrots and onions had been simmering for hours in a Crock-pot, covered with her favorite blend of dried onion soup mix and a couple cans of cream of mushroom soup. With a loaf of lemon bread rising and a cherry pie in the oven, she figured she'd earned her keep.

Oliver and Jake came through the kitchen, followed a few minutes later by Lane. "We've got to go out on the four-wheelers and hay the cattle," Jake said. "And we're going to bring a lot of the stock closer to the barns."

"What about supper?"

"We should be back in three, maybe four

hours." He handed out a yellow walkie-talkie to everyone. "Cell phone service isn't dependable out here. These are a little better, unless we get down into a ravine or beyond a mountain. But for where we'll be today, they should work. Call if you need to, and we'll check in as well."

He explained how to use the unit, then joined the other two at the back door where they bundled up into heavy coats and snow boots. He grinned at her as he stood in the open doorway. "You should take a break and go read by the fireplace for a while. I just got it going."

It was a suggestion too good to refuse.

As soon as they left, she curled up in a marshmallow-soft, ruby corduroy uphol-stered chair in front of the fireplace with a book and a cup of hot chocolate.

Even though it was just three in the af-ternoon, the house was darkened by the heavy snow falling outside. Gentle flames licked at the stack of logs, sending soft flickers of light through the room.

Lost in her novel, she only stirred to take the pie out of the oven and bake the bread. When she finally reached the end she leaned back in her chair with a sigh of satisfaction, then looked around in surprise.

The light outside was no longer gray and murky with the driving snow. It was pitch-black, and the fire had reduced to pulsing embers. The antique clock on the mantel read eight o'clock. Where was everyone?

She unwrapped herself from the comforter she'd found on the back of a chair and went to the kitchen to check on supper, then opened the back door and peered outside.

The wind escalated to a banshee shriek, quieted then screamed again, rattling the windows and doors. Blowing snow offered brief glimpses of the barns and security lights, but the barn lights were all off, so none of the guys were back yet. Were they lost? How easy would it be to become disoriented in the snow and darkness…or run out of gas somewhere and not know which direction to start trudging for home?

Worry nipping at her thoughts, she studied the slip of directions Jake had left and began calling each of the walkie-talkies, one by one.

No one answered.

"God—please keep them all safe," she murmured over and over as she paced through the house, uneasiness crawling up her spine like spider's legs. None of the first-floor windows had curtains and each one of them now seemed like a dark, menacing pit where someone standing outside could be hiding, watching her.

She made another round of the main floor, checking to be sure the windows and doors were locked, wishing that she'd thought to go to the barn and bring Maisie into the house before darkness fell and the storm hit.

The phone rang.

Relief rushed through her at the sound

of it. She raced back to the kitchen to the wall phone and picked up the receiver. "Hello?"

"Jake. Jake Kincaid." The voice was harsh and demanding.

"Wh-who is this?"

"Ahh." The voice softened to pure satisfaction, and then it laughed. The sound of it grated over her skin. "Well, well, well. What a surprise to find you there."

She pulled the receiver away from her ear and stared at it, revulsion crawling through her. She slammed it back in the cradle—but not fast enough to miss his final words.

"See you soon, sugar. Real, real soon."

FOURTEEN

Emma wrapped her arms around her waist, trying not to shake. She'd been afraid this would happen. And now she needed to get out of here fast—away from these kind, thoughtful people who didn't deserve the trouble she'd brought to their door.

Though she couldn't be sure, the voice had sounded like that of the man she'd found standing over Todd's body in her kitchen. All he'd had to do was go on the internet and trace Jake's license plate, then look his name up on Google to come up with directions straight to Jake's ranch.

In some ways, the internet was a terrible thing.

How far away was he? The caller ID had just read "Unavailable" but even so, area codes were no longer much help. Cell phones might originate from the owner's home area code, but that area code signified nothing about the owner's *current* location.

Maybe the guy was calling from Chicago or Denver or even in False Lake, but for the first time, she realized that the howling storm was a blessing. For now, the snow would preclude the possibility of him arriving anytime soon.

From outside came the sound of discordant engines pulling to a stop by the door. *Please, God, let it be Jake and the others.* Her heart hammering against her ribs, she stared at the kitchen entryway and backed slowly away, wondering where to hide.

But then, above the wind, she heard the sound of Jake shouting something and a moment later she heard him banging on the door.

She rushed over to unlock it, then stood aside as Oliver stumbled inside, bringing snow-laden wind with him. Jake followed, supporting Lane as they made their way straight over to the kitchen table without stopping to shuck off their boots.

Frozen blood covered the side of Lane's face.

"He got hurt," Jake said. "Bring me a basin of warm water and a clean washcloth."

"Stupid branch," Lane mumbled. "I didn't see it in the dark."

Emma filled a clean stainless steel mixing bowl with water and brought it over, then stood aside as Jake gently cleaned the wounds.

"We've got a first aid kit in the bathroom off the entryway. Could you get it?"

"I will." Oliver finished pulling off his coat and got the kit for him. "How does it look?"

"Head wounds always look worse than they really are." Jake opened up a packet of sterile gauze, poured out some antiseptic and continued dabbing at what appeared to be a deep scratch from Lane's temple up into his hairline.

"Ow!"

Lane leaned away, but Jake pulled him back. "Almost done. And luckily, this doesn't look bad enough for stitches. What do you two think?"

"All the way home, I was praying that this would be minor." Oliver leaned in close to study the wounds. "I think you're right. He isn't even bleeding anymore. You had me scared, Lane."

Emma took a look and nodded. "I agree with you both. What took you so long out there?"

"The weather turned worse." Oliver grabbed a tissue and blew his nose. "We had trouble getting the livestock moved and hay brought out. Then Lane disappeared and we couldn't find him. His four-wheeler was stuck in a drift."

"Only because I couldn't see a thing." Lane drew in breath. "When can we eat? I'm starved."

"Five minutes. It's been ready a long while, but with slow cookers it only means everything tastes better."

She quickly set the table and sliced up the homemade bread, then ladled the roast and vegetables onto a serving platter while Jake filled beverage glasses and Oliver shook a bag of Romaine lettuce salad mix into the big wooden salad bowl.

At the table, Emma bowed her head with the others as Oliver began a simple table prayer.

"Thank You for this wonderful food, God, for each other, and for all of our many blessings. Thank You for bringing us out of that storm safely. Please guard and protect all of us, in Jesus's name we pray. Amen."

She watched with a flicker of amusement as the three men dove into their meals. "Everything all right?"

"Great," Lane mumbled around a mouthful of lemon bread.

Oliver looked up at her over a forkful of tender roast.

"This definitely seals the deal as far as I'm concerned. You have a job for life if you want it."

"About that..." She took a deep breath, unsure of where to begin. "I need to borrow a four-wheeler or a snowmobile, if the roads are too bad for a truck."

Jake stopped cutting a bite of roast beef and looked up at her. "What's wrong?"

"I had a threatening call. A familiar voice—I think. If it's the guy who has been following me, then he knows where I am, Jake. It's time for me to leave before bad things happen here, and I don't want to be responsible for that."

Lane looked between them, clearly mystified. "What are you talking about?"

Jake ignored him. "What do you mean, you got a call? On your cell?"

"Worse. On your house phone. Which means someone has traced me here…and he probably knows where this ranch is. I don't know where he was calling from, but once the weather clears and the roads are all plowed, he could be here in a matter of time."

"Who?" Lane's voice escalated. "If you have some stupid, creepy boyfriend following you, you should stay here and *we'll* take care of him."

She managed a weary smile. "It's a little more complicated than that."

"But Lane is right. That guy might just hope he frightened you into running so he can get at you easier, when you're all alone." Oliver stabbed his fork in the air for emphasis. "You're much safer here."

"So you won't let me borrow a vehicle."

Oliver and Jake both shook their heads.

"That's a blizzard out there, in case you didn't know. You'd be lost in minutes and then you'd probably freeze to death." Oliver took another bite of the roast and sighed with pleasure. "Anyone who can cook like this has no business getting herself lost in the snow. Period."

Lane scowled. "So is this a boyfriend or what? You can at least tell me what's going on."

"Emma and her family witnessed a murder," Jake said. "Later, her mother died in a suspicious accident, and her father was murdered recently. Emma is afraid the same thing will happen to her. That's how we met, actually. She was on the run, and hiding from the men who are chasing her."

Lane turned his attention back to Emma. "So why don't you just go to the cops?"

"Back where I'm from, some of them were dirty. I've been afraid that they might have trumped-up charges against me, hoping I'd get picked up in some other jurisdiction and be sent right back to them.

I don't think I would survive if that happened."

"But Jake can help get this all straightened out. He was a good cop."

"I'm sure he was. But he isn't a cop now. And like I said, it isn't fair for me to stay any longer and put you all at risk."

"I'm working on this, Emma. I've got some good leads and I can help you, but I need more time. Don't throw this chance away."

"I appreciate what you're saying. But how could I live with myself if anything happened to one of you?"

"So you think we should let you go off and try to fend for yourself?" Oliver snorted. "Of course not. A man who won't defend a woman in need isn't worth his salt. We'll just need to keep our eyes open."

"I agree," Lane said. "Totally."

"Good. Next question. Emma, have you taken self-defense classes?"

"Just back in high school."

"What about weapons training?"

"No."

"Do you ride horses?"

"Not for a long time."

"Four-wheelers?"

She had to laugh at that. "Nope."

"Tomorrow the snow is supposed to end. We can go out behind the barns and do some target practice. Then I'll start giving you an extended education on transportation around here. You never know when an alternative might come in handy, and the horses and four-wheelers can be plain fun. Okay?"

"Maybe it would be easier to simply let me leave."

"Is that what you really want?"

He sounded so disappointed in her that she found herself shaking her head. "No. I just hope staying won't be a big mistake that gets someone killed."

After lunch the next day, Jake went through basic gun safety procedures over and over until Emma could recite them by heart. By the time he went through the process of cleaning, assembly and firing of the weapons he kept up at the house, her head was spinning.

Afterward, Lane joined them for an hour out behind the barn while she shot at paper targets fastened to bales of straw.

"This is going to take more than a single time," she warned when they finally headed back to the house to warm up.

"Of course it will. We can do some target practice every day until you feel comfortable. So what do you like the best so far?"

"The Glock G36, I think. The Ruger LCP was a nice size and shape for my hand, though. And I liked the .22 better than the shotgun. Less kick."

"See, you're starting to get the hang of it."

"I still wouldn't dream of whipping out some gun and trying to defend myself, though. I feel totally incompetent. And the thought of actually aiming at someone and pulling a trigger makes my blood go cold."

"You'd be surprised what you can do if your life depends on it. What if…someone had broken into your house?"

She shook her head.

"What if he was reaching for a gun and planned to shoot *you?*"

"I—I don't know. I hope I could. But I'd be second-guessing myself."

"What if he had a gun pointed at your child?"

She tried to imagine that moment. "That's easier. If I had a child, I guess I would do anything I could to keep him safe. *Anything.*"

"I hope you'll never have to use a weapon in self-defense, but given your situation I think it's wise to be ready. Understand?"

"Understood."

"I keep my weapons on the top shelf of

the closet at the back door of the house. What's the rule about the ammunition?"

"It's stored in your office. You never store them together, and never have either where a child could get at it."

"Good. Now, let's go saddle a horse, just for the fun of it."

Lane followed them to the barn. "You did really good," he said to her. "Jake worked with Maura for weeks but she never wanted anything to do with the guns. She finally refused to try."

"*She* probably didn't have any enemies," Emma said drily.

"Not any that were likely to shoot her, anyway."

Jake stopped in front of a stall and unbuckled the halter hanging from the stall front. "Here you go. Meet Buck."

"Me?" Emma hesitated, then took the halter and studied the straps, trying to remember which side was up. "I haven't done this since scout camp, you know."

He smiled. "Big hint—the long, unbuckled strap goes behind the ears."

"Gotcha." She walked into the stall, shut the door behind her and slowly approached the shoulder of the little buckskin gelding watching her with pricked ears. After her first failed attempt, she got the halter on him. "Right?"

"Right." Jake handed her a lead rope through the bars. "Use this. Try to never lead by just holding on to the halter. One jerk of the horse's head and he can break your hold and hightail it to the next county. The rope gives you a chance to reel him back in."

She led the horse out into the aisle and cross-tied him, then managed to saddle and bridle him under Jake's watchful eye.

"Perfect. After all that, you'd like to ride, wouldn't you?" Jake grinned at her. "Buck isn't much of a fireball, but he's dead broke and has a nice lope."

Her past two weeks had been filled with grief, fear and endless stress, but the moment Emma led the gelding out into the arena and swung into the saddle she felt the weight of all that emotion lifted from her shoulders.

Just as Jake had promised, Buck moved at a nice walk, then into a sweet, slow jog when she barely nudged him. After a few trips around the perimeter of the arena she touched her calf to his right side and he launched into an easy, rocking horse lope.

"He's so smooth I think I could bring a cup of coffee with me next time," she called out as she loped the little gelding past Lane and Jake. "I wish this would never end."

"You can ride anytime you want to," Jake said when she slowed down. "You don't even need to ask."

Lane and Jake went back into the horse barn, leaving her to walk the gelding a few times around the arena. When she finally stopped him and got off, she gave his neck a long hug, breathing in the scent of warm horse from his furry winter coat. "You are such a doll," she whispered.

He turned his head to rest it over her shoulder, as if returning her hug, and she felt her heart melt.

She'd started to lead Buck out of the arena, when she looked up and saw Lane and Jake watching from the tack room window. They were both grinning, then Lane gave Jake a high five.

She'd been set up, she realized. Set up to fall in love with a wonderful horse after an exhilarating ride, probably so she'd stop talking about leaving and just sit back and appreciate what she had here…at least for a little while longer.

It had certainly worked.

FIFTEEN

Jake had hoped Emma would fall for the little buckskin and realize that the ranch was the best place for her to stay, for the time being. All for her own good, of course, not because he had any personal interest.

He hadn't realized that seeing her out in the arena with Buck would affect him even more than it did her.

She had a natural, quiet seat on a horse and gentle hands, and Buck worked better for her than he ever had before, as if he was trying hard to please.

But it was when she got off and hugged

him, burying her head in his mane, that Jake had a glimpse into the true emotional trauma she must have been through during the past weeks. She'd lost *everything*. Her parents, her home, her job. She was such a petite, fragile little thing, yet she'd been running for her life, with no support system, for days.

He'd understood that on an intellectual level, but now he realized what it had cost her, and he wanted to do more than just help her escape her past. He wanted to go out there and take her in his arms and promise her that she'd never have to live in fear again. Promise that her enemies would disappear and she could be sheltered here forever, with people who cared about her.

Where had *that* come from?

He certainly had no business letting those ideas slip into his thoughts. Not while cattle rustlers and difficult loan officers were looming as major threats that could destroy the future of this ranch.

Those were the things he needed to concentrate on, not his growing attraction to a woman he was only trying to help.

And he didn't want responsibility for another person, at any rate. Not after the overwhelming disaster of his marriage to Maura, who had taken lying to the level of an art form, then left his heart in ruins. If he'd been so wrong about her, how could he trust his judgment again?

"You've been staring out the window at Emma for, like, ten whole minutes." Lane snickered and gave him a nudge. "Daydreaming?"

Jake pulled his thoughts back to the present. "Just thinking."

"I don't need to guess who you were thinking about. She's pretty, isn't she? Her hair isn't even pink anymore. And she's awfully nice."

"No idea what you're talking about, kid."

"Yeah, right." Lane made an elaborate show of looking at his wristwatch. "Guess

I'd better get up to the house and start my homework in case we have school tomorrow. And you'd better go help Emma get that saddle off. She might get hurt or something."

Lane was still laughing when he headed for the house.

After that mysterious call during the blizzard, Emma had been ready to flee. But two days passed, then three, without another word. Had that been the voice of one of the men pursuing her? Maybe not. Had the call been a fluke?

He hadn't actually called her by name. Maybe he'd been randomly flipping through a phone book, getting his kicks out of trying to scare people.

She prayed that was the case.

If it was, maybe she really was safe here, for a while. Maybe no one had seen Jake's license plate, or asked questions at the sales barn to find out who he was and where he lived. Maybe no one had realized that she left with him.

The thought was tantalizing…even if a small warning voice was reminding her that the arrival of danger was only a matter of time. Countless name and location changes over the past eighteen years had taught her that.

Yet with every passing day she felt herself sink into the fabric of ranch life a little more. Maybe she'd accidentally fallen into this job as a cook and a housekeeper, but she could almost pretend this was her family—and that she was living a normal, everyday life.

She rode horses with Lane and went target shooting with Jake, and even tried the four-wheelers a few times, bouncing down the plowed lane to the highway and back again, faster than she should have—a taste of the childhood she'd never had. A respite from her fear.

Now, on Sunday morning, she walked uncertainly into the community church with the Kincaid family and discovered yet another facet of small town life that she hadn't experienced, as people waved, and nodded, and came up to introduce themselves, welcoming her into their midst.

"Remember me?" A pretty redhead with twin toddlers tugging at her skirt stopped next to Emma and grinned. "Betsy, Pastor Will Anderson's wife. I'm so glad you've come to join us today."

"I am, too. This is such a lovely old church."

"Built in 1898, or so I'm told. Don't forget about the choir—we can sure use some more voices." One of the toddlers, a cute charmer in a pink ruffled dress, started to cry and Betsy bent to scoop her up. The little boy started to wail. "Sorry, you two. I can't hold you both." She sent an apologetic smile to Emma over her shoulder. "I guess I'd better get these rascals some juice."

Emma smiled, watching her herd the

twins toward a table set up with coffee and juice, and then she turned back to Jake. "I wonder—"

But he'd moved away and was talking quietly to a balding, heavyset man in the corner of the entryway. From the man's broad gestures and florid complexion, he didn't look happy.

"So you're still out at the Kincaid place? My, you must be quite the little cook."

The voice was sweet, laced with a touch of vinegar, and Emma didn't need to guess who it belonged to. She turned and found Maura behind her, dressed in a silky red sheath dress and short white fur jacket. "I'm not a great cook, but it's been fun trying."

"Interesting," Maura said, though her bored tone said otherwise. "So, what do you think of Jake?"

"I like my job a lot, actually. He's been good to work for."

"Then you don't know him well at all." She flicked a glance in Jake's direction.

"That's my father over there, Wayne Thurber. He's trying to talk some sense into him, but Jake is the most independent, stubborn man on the planet. I'll never understand why he doesn't simply take the money and run."

Uncomfortable with the woman's words, Emma scanned the crowd for Oliver and started to edge away. "I really wouldn't know anything about his business."

"Poor Jake. We'd still be married if he'd made better choices. But, if that land is so important to him, so be it." She gave a fluttery, dismissive wave of her hand. "I hope you're happier out there with him than I was."

"But I'm not— We're not—" Embarrassed, Emma glanced around and saw several women quickly avert their eyes. She felt her cheeks start to heat. "I'm a *housekeeper*. That's all."

Lane and Oliver materialized at her side, and Maura drifted away.

"I didn't understand a thing she said

about Jake, and then she assumed that I'm some sort of trollop."

"Just ignore her," Oliver said with a kindly smile. "We do."

"Her dad has wanted to buy Jake out for ages, to put up some high-end resort," Lane said. "And Maura wanted him to sell out so they could move to the Dallas suburbs where she could shop and stuff. But Jake won't let the ranch go no matter what anyone offers. It's been Kincaid land for generations."

"Thurber is rich and he's powerful, though. This is probably the only time anyone around here has stood up to the former senator over anything." Oliver chuckled. "It has probably done him some good."

Yet another of Jake's interesting facets, but Maura was entirely wrong. She thought he was stubborn. But a man who stuck to his principles and couldn't be bought was honorable; a man who wasn't cowed by someone of influence showed character.

And once again, Emma felt her admiration for him grow.

The cattle herds had been safe for a week. Long enough for Jake to let down his guard and skip some of his all-night vigils. But a half-dozen head were missing on Monday, then three on Tuesday. Like a slow hemorrhage, they were disappearing from random pastures. Jake now started taking turns with Oliver and Ed Feezer, the part-time ranch hand, at parking out along Highway 73 or on the various gravel roads that skirted sections of the Kincaid land. But wherever they parked, the nights stayed quiet. If cattle turned up missing it was from a distant side of the five-thousand acre spread.

Jake ran a weary hand across the dark stubble on his cheek when he walked into the house on Wednesday morning and slumped into one of the chairs at the kitchen table. "Sure smells good in here."

Emma looked up from the maple-cured sausage she was frying. He looked so exhausted that she wanted to walk over and give him a long, comforting embrace. Instead, she busied herself with pouring him a tall mug of black coffee and simply rested a hand on his shoulder when she set it in front of him. "How long can this go on?"

"Until we're bled dry, or we have a lucky break, I guess." He took a sip of coffee and closed his eyes. "If it continues like this I could end up defaulting on a big loan coming due on the thirty-first of March."

"None of the cattle have turned up at auction?"

"None. Which makes me wonder if they're being absorbed into other herds, or if they're being trucked far across the country to some small plant where the inspectors look the other way when stolen brands come through."

"And this ranch is still the only one being hit?"

"That I know of."

She brought him a glass of orange juice and a plate of poached eggs, sausage and whole grain toast. "I wonder why?"

"That's the question of the year." He drained half the glass of juice. "I need you to do me a favor today."

"Anything."

"The sheriff has sent out a number of notices about our thefts and our brand to the sales barns, livestock trucking companies and locker plants all over this part of the country. I'd like to blanket the smaller facilities again. You know, the smaller mom-and-pop-size businesses. I imagine they can be mighty busy, and the past notices could end up buried under a mountain of paperwork. I'll give you my old list and the flyer file, but if you search Montana locker plants and meat processing on the internet, you might turn up some I missed."

"I'll do it right after breakfast." She watched him take another bite of toast and then push his plate away. "Not hungry?"

"Just...tired. Sorry, Emma. It's all wonderful but I don't have much of an appetite. I'm going to bed for a couple hours."

Her heart aching for him, she cleared away his breakfast. As soon as Lane was off to school and Oliver was outside doing chores, Emma pulled out her laptop and logged onto the internet Yellow Pages.

In an hour she had more than a hundred physical addresses for the types of processing places Jake wanted to target, and of those, almost sixty percent had included a web address or at least an email address in their listing.

Impatient to get started, she designed a flyer and sent it off to every available email address she'd found, then sent her flyer file to the wireless printer in Jake's office to print a stack of hard copies. She began addressing business envelopes.

When she was finished stuffing them,

she tapped the envelopes into several neat
stacks and took them out to the mailbox
just as the rural carrier was arriving.

She watched the little white postal truck
turn around and head back toward town,
and then she looked skyward. *I've done
what I can, God, but we could sure use
some help here, before Jake ends up
losing everything. He's a good man, and
he has been so kind to me—please don't
let him fail.*

SIXTEEN

On Thursday afternoon, while Oliver and Jake were gone delivering a load of hay, Emma glanced out the window she was cleaning and did a double take. *Maura?*

It had been close to two weeks since the anonymous caller had terrified her. Two idyllic weeks of peace. Even so, she felt on edge whenever she went to town with Jake and Oliver, despite the fact that the people in town were warm and welcoming. The sound of the house phone ringing or a vehicle coming up the lane still had the power to make her heartbeat stumble.

Maybe things were quiet, but she had no

foolish illusions about the future. Someday, there would be a call. Or someone
would appear out of the shadows. And if
she wasn't alert enough, fast enough, she
would end up exactly like her parents.

From her first day here she'd known she
would eventually need to flee. But with
every passing day, she felt a deepening
bond with everyone here. With Oliver.
Lane. And especially with Jake, despite
her firm resolutions to keep her distance.

But now, the little red sports car zoom-
ing up the snowy lane only spelled trouble
of the awkward kind, because the blonde
at the wheel vacillated between being
subtly catty and overly solicitous, and
Emma only wanted to be left alone.

She grabbed a jacket and went outside
to meet Maura at her car door. "I'm afraid
Jake isn't here. But I can tell him you
stopped and ask him to call you."

"I knew he was gone. I saw his truck
heading out of town." Maura bit her full
lower lip.

Something was different about her today—less brittle, less superior, maybe. If Emma hadn't known better, she might have thought she detected a hint of fear in the woman's big blue china-doll eyes.

"Can I help you?"

Lines of tension formed between her delicately arched eyebrows. "You can help Jake. I know he won't listen to me."

Emma folded her arms across her middle to ward off the chilly breeze. "I just work here. I don't have any special influence."

A smile briefly touched her lips. "Really. Then either you're blind or I am, because I *saw* how he was looking at you at church."

He'd probably been his usual protective self, but *that* topic had no place outside of the people who lived here. "I'm sure you're wrong, but give me your message and I'll give it to him."

"Tell him…tell him to be careful."

Emma blinked.

"I've heard talk around town about Jake's stolen cattle. I've heard that someone has some kind of vendetta against him, and that the situation could escalate. That...that he could get hurt."

"*Who* is saying those things? Did you tell the sheriff?"

Maura drew back. "It's just gossip, Emma. You can't get someone arrested for that."

"But it sounds like a threat, and that had to come from somewhere."

"I—I shouldn't have come here." She shifted her car into Drive. "I'm sorry—I should go."

"Wait. You said I could help him. What could I possibly do?"

"Tell him to leave. Pack up, sell out and just go."

"This is where he grew up, Maura."

Maura stared at her steering wheel for a long moment, then looked up at Emma with tears sparkling in her eyes. "You probably heard about the end of our marriage. *Why* it ended."

"I don't think Jake is the type to ever talk about things like that."

"I got the idea that I couldn't live out here, on a struggling ranch. I wanted travel. Beautiful clothes. Money. And I cheated on him to find what I thought was my dream. I'd give anything to go back and be able to make much different decisions, Emma." She took a deep breath. "I can't. But I still care about what happens to him, and I'm pretty sure there's going to be trouble. Please—do what you can to make him leave."

Jake pulled up next to the barn and rested his wrists on the top of the steering wheel. "Even though we got that semiload of hay delivered, we're still in the hole this month. I just hope the horse sale on the twenty-third goes well."

Oliver nodded. "It will. Early spring is the perfect time of year for a horse sale, and that one has been drawing bidders from across the country every year. You should do well at the cattle sale, too. Everything will work out."

"I'd like to believe it."

Oliver waggled an eyebrow. "Maybe you'll even start thinking about settling down again, once all of this blows over."

"Not in this lifetime. I—"

His phone rang. He glanced at the unfamiliar number on the caller ID, debated, then took the call. Oliver was halfway to the barn when Jake disconnected, then flung open his truck door. "Oliver—we've got to go. *Now*. I just got a call from a meat locker. They said they received one of Emma's flyers, and they think they have one of our cows. The guy who brought it in is still there, and they're going to try to keep him talking."

"What about the sheriff?"

"I told them to call that number, too."

The locker facility was on the farside of Walker, a tiny mountain town over thirty miles away. The trip seemed to take forever, though Jake pushed the truck to seventy miles an hour. This was the break he'd been praying for…one that could lead to resolving the entire cattle rustling operation that was bleeding his ranch dry.

But if the suspect got suspicious and took off, they'd bc back to square one. Please, God, let him still be there.

The GPS in the truck led them down a narrow, twisting road outside of Walker, then into a grove of trees where a couple of cars, plus a truck and stock trailer were nosed up to a concrete block building with holding pens off to one side.

Jake pulled in behind the trailer, blocking its exit.

"I hope this is our guy," Oliver said. "What do you want me to do?"

"Just stay out here and watch for anyone trying to escape. Use your cell to call mine if you see anything at all suspicious."

Jake's blood hummed in his veins as he sauntered into the building, prepared to take down the first man who started to run.

But disappointment arrowed through him when he stepped inside the small retail area off the front entryway and only found a man in a blood-stained apron with "Ritchie" embroidered on the pocket, and a stocky older woman sitting with a gray-haired fellow in his mid-seventies, who held a cane crossways on his lap.

The man in the apron gave Jake a quick once-over. "Are you the fellow we called about…um…meat processing?"

Jake nodded.

"Come on back." He led the way down a cement hallway to a holding pen and flipped on the lights. "You are Jake Kincaid. Right?"

Jake nodded.

"Then take a look at that angus heifer over there." He pulled a piece of paper from his back pocket and unfolded it. "I think that brand matches the one on this flyer."

Jake climbed over the high wooden fence and held out his arms to drive her into the opposite corner of the pen. Sure enough, the Rocking K brand of the Kincaid Ranch was on her shoulder. He stared at it, feeling a mixture of relief and excitement. "She's mine all right. Did you call the sheriff?"

"Yep. Right after you and I talked."

"How long ago did the guy leave? Did you get his license plate?"

The man's forehead knit together in a frown. "You just walked past him—the old guy with a cane, talking to my wife. But honestly, if *he's* a cattle rustler, I'm one of those hippy vegee-tarians. And that's a fact."

"Yet he's in possession of stolen cattle. I think he and I need to have a little chat."

Out in the sitting area, the woman stood up and moved aside when Jake walked in. She wrung her hands nervously as she went to stand by Ritchie. "This is Mr. Nelson, a new customer of ours," she said.

"Can I get you a cup of coffee, or something?"

"I'm fine." Jake took the chair she'd just vacated. "A fine winter's day, isn't it?"

The old gent nodded.

"You've got a nice heifer back there. Are you planning to keep all the meat, or will you be wanting to sell a half?"

"It's not for sale." He frowned a little. "Our son-in-law gave it to us. We're splitting it with our other daughter's family once it's all cut and packaged. Times have been hard lately, so it's a gift we can sure use."

"I'd be interested, if he has any more where this one came from. There's nothing like a good angus steak."

"He says he has a big herd, all right. Who are you?"

"Just an interested buyer, and I'll pay top dollar," Jake drawled. "Give me his name and number, and I'll look him up."

"You don't need to go calling him. Ed's

going to be here in about a half hour with a steer of his own."

"Ed?" Jake stared at him. "Ed Feezer?"

Nodding, the old man stood. "But I can't stick around for introductions. I gotta get back home."

"No problem. I'll just wait around and see if I can make a deal." Jake added a lazy, good-ole-boy grin for good measure, but it was all he could do to keep it in place as he sauntered outside and watched the man drive away.

Deputy Gene Kirby arrived just minutes later. Jake met him at his patrol car and filled in both him and Oliver on what he'd learned. "I can't believe Ed Feezer would do a thing like this, to be honest. I don't think his father-in-law has a clue about the stolen beef, but I'm going to take care of this here and now."

"Whoa, Jake—you might have been the law when you were working down in Wyoming, but you'd better leave this up to me. You don't want to get yourself in trouble."

"I don't plan on doing anything stupid." Jake looked around. "I think we should all park our vehicles out back so Ed doesn't see them and get spooked."

The deputy nodded. "I'll call for backup."

"Suit yourself. I just want to be here when he turns up with a stolen heifer, so he can find out how I feel about being betrayed."

Jake pulled to a stop behind the locker plant, anger still simmering through him.

"You're going to listen to that deputy, right? You aren't going to do anything stupid." Oliver regarded him with concern. "The whole point is making sure Ed gives the location of your cattle, then is arrested and tried. You need to get your cattle back, not go after vengeance."

"I know. But I can't believe what we've all been through at the ranch. The long nights. The worries. And Ed knew it—he even helped us stand guard. Yet all the time, he knew exactly what was going on. Unbelievable."

"This ought to be interesting." Oliver glanced in the side mirror at the patrol car now parked next to the truck. Gene was still inside, talking on his radio and gesturing expansively. "You think Kirby will give you some breathing room like you asked?"

"It's his business, I guess. At least there aren't a lot of people around so we can keep this private." Jake unbuckled his scat belt, pulled a flashlight out of the glove box, then climbed out of the truck and leaned against the hood.

Sure enough, a few minutes later, a truck with a bad muffler and a trailer rumbled off the highway and jounced, leaf springs creaking, across the rutted gravel on the front side of the building.

It pulled to a stop. A truck door squealed open and slammed shut.

Jake waited for the jingle of the bells mounted above the front entrance, then rounded the building and jogged to the stock trailer parked near the loading chute. He walked around it, with Deputy Kirby at his heels, peering through the horizontal metal slats and sweeping the interior with the flashlight beam until he finally got a good look at the brand on the heifer's shoulder.

"So, is it yours?" Oliver stood back a few yards, keeping an eye on the front door of the building.

"Definitely."

"Then let me take care of this, son." Kirby looked up from the notes he was writing on his clipboard. "There'll be time enough for you to talk to him, later."

"No. I'm going to handle it. Just give Oliver and me a couple minutes, then come on in." Jake strode through the cluttered front retail area of the locker plant and went on to the back office, where a thin, wiry man in overalls stood talking to the owner. "Hey, Ed."

Ed spun around, his face draining from ruddy to pale in an instant. "Jake!"

"Looks like you're keeping busy."

Ed's gaze shifted between Oliver and Jake. "I guess. Ranch work is slow, but I've been picking up hours at the body shop."

"Must be going well. I see you're butchering a real nice heifer."

"A man's gotta eat."

"From what I hear, your family has been eating pretty well, lately."

Ed paled even further, gleaming beads of perspiration forming on his forehead. "I have a little place. Run a few head of cattle of my own."

"Interesting choice of brand, then. Real similar to mine."

"Is it? I guess that's how she came. When I bought her. In—" He swallowed hard. "Back in…October."

"You've had her that long?"

Ed nodded a little too forcefully. "Yep, October."

"You worked twenty years for my father and now you've worked over three for me. We've tried to treat you fair. How long have you been stealing our cattle?"

He fidgeted with his keys. "Not ever. I swear."

"Oh, I certainly believe you—you being such an upstanding citizen and all. Where are they, Ed? We've lost sixty-three cattle over the past two months. Since you know everything about our beef program and where the herds are at any given time, it must have been awfully easy to steal them. Now I want every last one of them back. If they've gone to slaughter then I want every dime you got for them."

Ed's jaw quivered. "I don't have your cattle. You can go search my place."

"That's odd, because I just found your father-in-law with another one of them at this meat locker. The Rocking K brand was clear."

"It was the first time. He just let me have a couple—" Ed's mouth clamped shut.

"Who did?" Jake dropped his voice to a low, silky note. "Your *father-in-law?*"

"No. Not him." His jaw working, Ed's face turned a dark red.

"Well, I'm flat confused. You are in possession of my heifer and Mr. Nelson says you have a lot more. Who else is involved in this, Ed?"

He fell into a stony silence.

"You do understand the current law, correct? You're facing ten years in prison and up to a fifty thousand dollar fine. Anything used in the theft—trucks, trailers— can be confiscated. And frankly, the fact that you could betray me like this makes me want to see that you are prosecuted to the full extent of the law."

A door behind them swung open with a squeak and Kirby walked in. If anything, Ed grew even more agitated at the sight of a deputy, his face mottled and sweat dripped down his temples.

Jake stepped aside. "He's all yours. Apparently he's the only one responsible. I want separate charges filed for each head of cattle he stole, because it wasn't just one theft. He did it multiple times."

The deputy pulled a pair of handcuffs from a leather pocket hanging from his belt, cuffed Ed and read him his Miranda rights, then started marching him away.

"Wait—wait." Ed balked at the door. "It *wasn't* just me. I didn't even do any of the hauling."

"You do understand the rights I just read you? That you can request the presence of your lawyer if you say anything to me?"

He nodded grimly. "I'm not saying nothin', understand? Except if I was you, I'd pay Wayne Thurber a visit…and I'd do it fast."

Outside the shop, Oliver stood next to Jake and watched the deputy shove Ed into the backseat of his patrol car. "Where did you come up with 'separate charges for each head of beef'?"

"Sounded more impressive. And I do think Ed was impressed."

"What was that about Senator Thurber?" Oliver shook his head.

"*Former* Senator Thurber. I'm not so sure it's as crazy as you might think."

"Just because he's been wanting to buy you out? No man in his right mind would risk his reputation and his future by going that far for a piece of land."

"If he knew he could get away with it? Running me into bankruptcy would lead to a foreclosure sale and a mighty big opportunity to pick up the best scenic land this side of the Rockies. Maura said he had plans to build one of the most luxurious resorts in this part of the country."

"But he was your *father-in-law.*"

"Was. And there was no love lost between us. I wasn't good enough to marry his daughter, and then it was all my fault when the marriage crashed. Remember?"

After checking the patrol car door locks—which only opened from the outside—the deputy strolled back to Jake and shook his head. "What's he on, meth? That's about as crazy a story as I've heard."

"Maybe. But if I were you, I'd definitely check it out. And I definitely wouldn't go alone."

SEVENTEEN

Maura's words played through Emma's thoughts endlessly as she tried to keep busy at the ranch, but every few minutes she glanced at the clock and felt a niggle of fear. Lane was in town at a high school basketball game and she knew he wouldn't be back until around ten. But where were Jake and Oliver?

She'd seen them come back with a truck and flatbed trailer after selling a load of hay while she was starting to work on supper, then suddenly they'd dropped the trailer in front of the barn and took off, and neither one was answering his cell phone.

She'd had a hard time believing Maura's warning—it had seemed so overly dramatic given this quiet ranching area and the fact that Jake seemed to be a man who handled trouble with such quiet assurance. But now, with supper still in the oven on Low to stay warm and dusk fading into darkness, her worries were starting to grow.

The phone had rung three times in the past hour, but the caller hung up when she answered. *What if Maura was right?*

Her eyes fell on the lovely old embroidered Bible verse on the living room wall, which Oliver said had been done by Jake's grandmother.

Don't worry about anything; instead, pray about everything. Tell God what you need, and thank Him for what He has done. If you do this, you will experience God's peace, which is far more wonderful than the human mind can understand. His peace will guard your hearts and minds as you live in Christ Jesus. Philippians 4:6–7

She'd seen it a hundred times, passing through the living room, but she hadn't stopped to read it. Now the words seemed to fill her heart with warm reassurance. How many times in her life had she been swamped with fear and uncertainty, feeling so alone?

She prayed—mostly when she was in trouble—and she went to church when she could even though frequent moves had meant she never really became a part of any one church family, but had she ever really fully placed herself in God's hands and trusted that everything would be all right?

The phone rang.

Her heartbeat stumbled as she moved to answer it, her hand hovering over the phone. It *could* be Jake…couldn't it?

She picked up the receiver. "Hello?"

No one was there.

Okay, God...I so need Your help, here. Please, please keep Jake and Oliver safe, wherever they are. Thank you for bringing me here, where I'm no longer so totally alone...but please, bring me that sense of peace. I'm so tired of being afraid.

The phone rang again.

Lane came home at a quarter to eleven and disappeared into his room. Jake finally called, a few minutes later, and said he and Oliver would be back in an hour. He sounded tense and she'd wanted to ask what was going on, but at least she'd heard his voice and he had to be okay.

She wandered through the house, too uneasy to go to sleep, too unsettled to read. The hallway leading to a bathroom and the main floor bedrooms was a veritable family gallery, with dozens of lovingly framed photographs cataloging the passing years. She wistfully studied them all.

Jake and his sister in a sandbox. School

photos throughout grade school. On the swingset in the back of the house. Proudly standing with their 4-H calves and horses at what appeared to be the county fair.

And later, standing with prom dates. High school graduation. Every important step recorded, framed and lovingly displayed. She wondered what it felt like, to have such solid assurance of belonging somewhere. To someone. To have a family, a history.

Her own childhood photographs had been lost—perhaps had never existed. After her adoption there had been the requisite school photos, but after so many moves, some made in haste, they were long gone.

The back door opened and footsteps stomped into the kitchen. She heard Jake's and Oliver's hushed voices. Relief rushed through her as she hurried to the kitchen.

"Is everything okay? Maura was here and said some crazy things and I've been so worried about you two ever since. I tried calling but neither of you answered. Did you get my messages?"

Oliver and Jake exchanged glances.

"We were out of range, probably. Then things got a little busy and I haven't listened to any." Jake hung his jacket on a peg by the door. "What did she say?"

"Something about your cattle and someone having a vendetta against you. And how you should sell out and leave before you got hurt."

"So she knew," Jake said heavily, looking at Oliver. "And she probably knew for some time, yet she never said a single word."

"You know Wayne, though. He probably held something over her head."

"Like her trust fund, probably. *That* would get her attention."

Oliver shucked off his boots and coat, and went to the refrigerator to peer inside.

"I had supper on warm for hours, but I finally had to pitch it. Can I make you soup and sandwiches? Leftover lasagna from last night?"

"Nah. I think I'll just turn in. It's been a long night. But a good one. Right, Jake?"

He padded away in his stocking feet, his face gray and drawn. He looked as if he'd aged ten years since she last saw him. "What happened?"

Jake leaned a shoulder against the refrigerator. "Your flyers helped end the cattle rustling, Emma. Tomorrow I think we should all take you out for a big dinner."

"You found the cattle?"

"And the men responsible. Ed Feezer has worked here on and off for years, and he helped engineer the whole thing, but Maura's father was behind it. If we hadn't gotten a lead today from a locker plant, we wouldn't have been able to catch the semiloads of cattle being sent to Thurber's ranch in south Texas tonight."

She stared at him. "But…but I thought the family was wealthy. *Why?*"

"He's been after this ranch for years,

and apparently has been promising a group of investors that he'd be able to start work on a multimillion dollar resort here. They were getting impatient, applying a lot of pressure to get their money back, and he probably figured running me into bankruptcy would be the most expedient move."

"Unbelievable."

Jake's laugh sounded bitter. "I wouldn't be surprised if the bank will now be more reasonable about my loans, if he isn't around to pressure someone there."

"But a *senator*..." she mused, still not quite believing it.

"That doesn't mean he's honorable. And given the way he ranted at the sheriff tonight, I wouldn't be surprised if there's an element of early onset dementia there, too. Once he got angry, not many of his words made sense. They actually took him to the hospital, instead of booking him at the county jail."

"Oh, Jake…I'm so glad all of that is over."

He looked so weary that she wanted to wrap her arms around him, but caught between impulse and propriety, she hesitated.

He must have had the same idea, though, because a grin touched his lips and his eyes seemed to darken. "Come here," he said in a low voice. He wrapped his arms around her and tucked her head beneath his chin. "After everything that happened tonight, I could sure use a hug."

Me, too, she thought. *Me, too.* She melted against his hard muscled chest, savoring the warmth of him and the steady beat of his heart, and realized that she had wanted this impossible moment from the day they'd met.

EIGHTEEN

Thoughts of that embrace filled Emma's mind and threatened to break her heart as she moved through the next two days. Jake was everything she'd ever dreamed of, but the impossibility of staying here weighed more heavily on her with every passing day.

She could have no future here. It wouldn't be fair. She could never be sure that she was truly free of her past. Someone could appear out of the blue and the very people she loved could lose their lives because of her. And that terrible possibility was no part of her imagination. Not after burying two parents and seeing Todd Hlavicek dead on her kitchen floor.

It was time to leave.

She made her daily call to Doris at the post office.

"Hi. This is—"

"Goodness gracious, I know who this is, Emma. I've put a trace on your mail twice, and I just followed up on it today. If it's not at Deer Lodge and not here, it should have gone to the Mail Recovery Center in St. Paul."

"Where they'd throw it away?"

"Only if it's scanned and deemed worth less than ten dollars, and if it can't be forwarded to the owner."

She closed her eyes. What kind of value would they place on the documents she'd sent? Worse than discarding it all, what if they turned it all over to the police?

"But you sent these things by registered mail and they keep something like that for at least ninety days," Doris added. "I sent them a description and the dimensions of the boxes in case the label was damaged. I just keep wondering if your package was in the semi that was in the accident."

"If…if I were to leave town and kept in touch, could you forward them to my next address if they ever turned up?"

"Of course, dear. But don't tell me you're leaving!"

"I've been here longer than I should already. I…um…had other plans before ever coming to False Lake."

Doris clucked her tongue. "And here we all thought you and Jake might just be a good match. How his ex-wife treated him *still* makes me angry. And you seem like such a sweet girl."

But Emma could well imagine what the older woman would say if Emma brought tragedy to the Kincaid ranch.

She had very little to pack in the duffel bag that she'd picked up on one of her trips to town. The clothes she'd bought at the Walmart in Colorado. The few things she'd purchased up at the consignment shop in False Lake. If anything, the past month had taught her that she could survive with few possessions, and that traveling light made transitions a lot easier.

Tomorrow morning, she would ask Oliver or Jake for a ride to the bus stop in the next town beyond False Lake, and then she would be on her way.

Distracted, Emma pulled together a supper of wine-braised beef tips, glazed baby carrots and mashed potatoes like her mom had made—loaded with sour cream, cream cheese and onion salt.

She put the last serving bowl on the table, lit a candle in the center, and then watched Jake, Lane and Oliver take their usual places, feelings of nostalgia already weighing heavily on her heart. This would be her last night here.

Jake looked up at her after they said grace, his eyes warm with concern. "Is something wrong?"

"Just thinking." The men had been busy over the past couple days, hauling the cattle home from one of the most remote pastures on Thurber's ten-thousand acre ranch, so she hadn't seen them much. She looked at each one in turn. "I'm thinking that you guys are pretty special people. I've really appreciated the chance to be here."

Oliver leaned back in his chair and frowned. "That sounds like a farewell."

"It's time, Oliver."

"Maybe not." Jake put his fork down. "What would you say if I told you there was no connection between the knife I found near where you were attacked at the sale barn, and that break-in at your motel?"

Lane's mouth dropped open. "Knife? *What* knife?"

She stared at Jake. "They weren't the same? You're *sure?*"

"I heard from Megan this afternoon before we went out to hay the cattle. She got results back on the knife, and then contacted the police in Denver to check on the prints lifted at the motel. Not a match."

Lane's eyes rounded. "This is like *CSI!*"

"All this time, I was convinced it had to be the same guy."

"Nope. The barn hand was telling the truth, apparently."

"Was either set of prints in the AFIS system?"

"That's where it gets interesting. The prints at the hotel match a man named Victor Marquesa. He has a rap sheet that reads like a novel, and he's known to have done contract work for the Rodriguez family."

Emma closed her eyes. "Contract. As in..."

Jake nodded. "Murder for hire."

"Was...was he the man who killed my dad?"

"If he was caught and he still had the gun, they could check ballistics on it, and maybe there'd be an answer. But a guy like him would know enough to use a random gun and wipe it clean, then ditch it."

"Does Megan have any police photos of him?"

"She said she found some in the system from his previous arrests and she'll email one. It's probably in my in-box now. I'll print off copies for us, and I'll send one on to the sheriff's department so they can give it to their deputies and all of the surrounding counties."

Lane's eyes gleamed with excitement. "Maybe we can post pictures all over town. Like at the feed store, the grocery and so on. Not wanted posters. Just 'if you see this man, please call this number.' What do you think?"

"We can check with the sheriff on that." Jake took a slow sip of coffee. "At least now we have a face and a name, Emma. That makes it a lot easier, instead of just jumping at shadows and wondering who you can trust. When we take this guy down you can finally relax."

She smiled sadly. "What would be the charges against him if there's no proof he killed my dad? Nothing much that would stick, and then he'd be free again. And if it isn't him out there, there could be someone else—and someone else after that. As long as Eduardo Rodriguez draws breath I'll still never know when my last day is coming."

"None of us do," Jake said gently. "But I'm working on this. And I promise you that soon it will all be over."

The photo of Victor Marquesa arrived by email before supper. Jake brought it out and passed it around after she cleared the table and brought out still-warm chocolate chip cookies for dessert.

"Does he look familiar? Have you seen him around town?"

Lane and Oliver studied the photo and shook their heads.

Emma stared at it, unable to tear her gaze away.

It was a booking shot from some police station, with a string of numbers on a strip across the man's chest. He stared straight at the camera, his mouth set in a hard line. His tangled hair appeared long and greasy, and there were dark shadows under his deep-set eyes.

"What about you, Emma? Does he look anything like one of the men you saw in your house?"

"With his hair cut short and washed, maybe. If he weighed twenty or thirty pounds more...maybe. I just don't know."

"I'm not sure myself if he's the man who approached me at that Ogallala truck stop. He was wearing a hat low over his forehead, and it was dark. But whether you recognize him or not, this man nearly got to you, Emma. The fingerprints prove it. Tomorrow we're going to get even more serious about finding ways you can protect yourself. Deal?"

She hesitated, thinking about her packed duffel bag.

The eyes of the man in the photo were cold, flat, lifeless, with a reptilian lack of emotion that chilled her blood. What were the chances that she could fend off a man like this one?

Jake had to be kidding if he was suggesting that she had any real chance at all.

She dropped her gaze and prepared to tell the biggest whopper of her entire life. "I—I'm just not cut out for life on a ranch. I'm a lot happier with city life. I'll stay a couple more days, long enough for you to advertise for a new housekeeper. But then I really need to leave."

NINETEEN

Jake stood at the back door of the barn and stared out into the night. Tonight was clear, the sky filled with stars, the snow changed to diamonds under the moonlight. To the west, the ghostly images of the soaring, snow-covered peaks of the Rockies were barely visible as gray on black.

Beautiful.

Awe-inspiring.

And he'd never felt so lonely in his life.

He'd been charmed and attracted to Emma from that first day they'd met, even if he'd refused to admit it to himself. But when had his feelings grown into something that had taken hold of his heart and wouldn't let go?

The inadvertent touches as they passed a platter at meals, the shared glances of amusement at something Lane said, the moments of wonder at a newborn foal or Maisie's antics had somehow coalesced into something much deeper when he hadn't been looking. And there it was, as undeniable as the moon overhead.

But now she was planning to leave.

Her words after supper had brought back all the pain of the day Maura walked out on him. The disbelief. The bargaining. The argument that ended when she threw her purse across the front seat of her car and drove away.

What would happen to Emma if she left? Would he ever find out, or would he always wonder?

He pulled his cell phone from his belt and scrolled through his contacts list, then touched a name and number. Calling every day hadn't endeared him to his quarry, but sometimes being a thorn was more effective than playing nice.

Please, God, help make this happen.

A man's voice answered, sleepy and irritable, and supremely fed up.

And fifteen minutes later, Jake was driving to the airport in Billings far faster than the speed limit allowed.

Friday dawned clear and cold, as gray and dreary as the feeling in Emma's heart. Jake had been gone forty-eight hours now, after leaving only a terse note saying, *Back soon—tell Emma not to leave.*

What did that mean?

Some sort of business trip, and he just wanted her to stick around so he could say farewell? Or that he was just worried for her safety and didn't want her to leave at all? That wasn't news. She'd told him she didn't want to stay here and, by default, her words had let him know that he didn't matter to her, either. He hadn't said a word in response. He was probably relieved she'd said it first.

Oliver stood at the kitchen windows facing the barn, his hands braced on his lower back. "They say an ice storm is headed this way. A bad one. Guess I'd better go out and do chores early."

"Oliver, I hate to ask when you're so busy, but I could use a ride to Masonville. Or if you don't have time to spare, maybe I could borrow one of the pickups."

"You need to go to town for groceries?"

"I need to get to the bus stop. The Greyhound comes through at 4:35 p.m. If I took a pickup, I could leave it there and lock it up safely so you could go get it later."

"Oh, honey—don't go now. Jake isn't back, and—"

"I don't think he would mind a bit. He's been gone for two days without a single word. He probably thinks I'm long gone."

"He cares for you. I know he does. The fact that anyone could even think about harming you just tears him up."

She tried for a smile. "He hides it rather well."

"When Maura left, it almost killed him. His parents loved each other until the day they died, and that's how he thought marriage should be. Until you showed up I figured he'd never take that risk again." His piercing gaze seemed to see straight into her heart. "And if I'm not mistaken, you have feelings for him, too."

"It isn't that. I…" She turned away to gather her purse and her duffel bag, unable to face him any longer. "I just want to leave. I'll leave the truck at the Greyhound stop in front of the Dalton Drugstore. Okay? Otherwise I'll need to hitchhike, and that just doesn't seem like a smart thing to do."

Jake walked along the cold, cement block hallway with the guard, feeling dozens of eyes on him.

Security cameras were mounted on the ceiling every ten feet and he had no doubt that every movement was being recorded as well as watched in real time. He'd been through three checkpoints and one body scan station reminiscent of those in airports already, and ahead, there was another triple set of locked doors fabricated of bulletproof glass.

So no one could lay in wait behind them, he supposed, though with this level of maximum security any attempt at escape would be useless.

The guard took him through the three doors, then to an open area framed with glass walls and divided down the center by a long aluminum table, with a thick glass barrier running down the center of the table. Steel quarter-inch mesh occluded the small spaces left open for conversation.

The setup was worthy of some ox of a cold-blooded killer who might tear apart an unlikely visitor, à la Hannibal Lecter, but the small, frail Latino male shuffling into the room from the opposite corner looked barely strong enough to support the thick shackles at his ankles and wrists.

The guard nodded at the center of the room. "Sit. Do not touch the barrier in any way. Keep your hands on the table. Understood? You've got ten minutes."

Jake waited for the wizened old man to sit, as a gesture of respect, then took his own seat. "Mr. Rodriguez, thank you for this visit. I understand you choose only to see some family members and your lawyers."

"There is no point." He squinted at Jake, sizing him up. "You are a cop."

Surprised, Jake nodded. The man's face was as wrinkled and brown as a shrunken apple, but the glitter in his eyes was sharp and watchful, and Jake guessed that he missed nothing. "I was, but just when I was living in Wyoming. Never Chicago."

Rodriguez bared his teeth in a smile. "Then we never met on a…*professional* basis."

"No. I've come about some witnesses at your trial eighteen years ago."

"You're going to tell me that they lied and now I will be free?" His rusty laugh filled the room. "No. I think not."

"It was a family. A couple, and their young daughter. They were called as witnesses in the trial, and testified about seeing the murder of Congressmen Whitler in a Washington, D.C., parking garage. The killers were found, and the connection traced to you."

Rodriguez shrugged. "So they said. I say it was not that way. Two thugs, very poor choice of target. It became a way to send me to this place where I now wait to die. I was guilty of many crimes, and I have asked God's forgiveness. But that was one thing I did not do."

"That investigation brought down the top levels of your organization for murder. Murder for hire. Drug trafficking. Extortion. Many of your lieutenants were convicted, but now some are being released as their sentences end."

"Perhaps they have changed their ways."

"The thing is, this particular family that was called to testify at your trial is now being hunted down, one by one. The mother was killed in a suspicious car accident. The father was gunned down in a parking lot recently. Since then, their daughter has been on the run, pursued by someone."

"And you think I am seeking vengeance. Destroying my enemies."

"Someone is after this young woman. She didn't want to witness a murder, and she suffered from nightmares for years afterward. She didn't want to speak up at the trial, but she had to. I'm trying to help her, and I think we've identified at least one man who has been after her. But I wonder if there are more—and when this will come to an end."

"And you think I could do this from these prison walls. What would I gain?

No, it is not my doing. I grew up in the church as a boy. I fell away, but being in this place and knowing I will die soon has given me a new perspective. I have no family left to provide for. No reason to eliminate enemies I have forgiven."

He was a hardened criminal, and the number of deaths he'd ordered had probably never been fully counted. He'd been the head of an international drug cartel. But looking into his guileless face now, Jake almost believed him—until he caught a brief, cunning glint in the man's eyes.

"Then if the murders of this woman's parents weren't ordered by you, is there someone else?"

"I have no hand in the business anymore."

"I heard otherwise."

A small, satisfied smile briefly touched the old man's slack mouth. "There was a time, yes, that might be true. Even from behind these walls. But that was long ago. Now? There is no point. My sons are all dead, through the violence of the drug wars in northern Mexico. I'll never walk as a free man again and I would never enjoy the profit. So why would I care?"

"What about others in your organization?"

"My associates? Eh—that is hard to say. Some might have, as they say, delusions of grandeur. But it will only lead to death. Rivals in this business are not pleasant men."

"There are rumors that you still have great wealth hidden away...and that some of those 'associates' might do anything they can to get their hands on it." Jake chose his words carefully. "I believe the witness who was recently killed may have performed services for you...handling money, investments."

Rodriguez said nothing for a long moment.

"Please."

The old man shrugged dismissively. "Baker. He was known as Baker, then.

There were rumors that he and his family went into witness protection after my trial. But that meant nothing to me."

Jake lifted a brow in disbelief. "You had no interest in paying back the family that helped put you here?"

A flash of something dark and chilling twisted Rodriguez's features. "Finding a man such as Baker can be…impossible, when the government chooses to hide him well. After a time, the benefit is no longer worth the cost, eh? It would serve no purpose except to avenge my honor."

So Rodriguez *had* tried, and failed.

"Is it possible that any of your former associates might think that Baker and his family knew where your fortune was hidden, and that they tried to force him to disclose the information?"

"Anything is possible. But there is no money. Why would I keep it? Like I said, I am an old man who is going to die. I have no children. I spent millions on my defense and on that of my…friends.

Most of them became traitors. The rest of my money went to a church in southern Mexico, where the nuns take in the poor and the hungry."

It hit Jake then that for Rodriguez, this conversation was little more than a game; a skillful fabrication of truth and lies that provided him with a chance for amusement. A diversion, and nothing more. Which still left Jake with no concrete answers, and the clock was ticking.

The guard at the side of the room held up his wrist and tapped his watch, then held up two fingers.

"Just one last question. Four of your associates were released in the past year. Did any of them know about Baker?"

Jake rattled off a list of the names, then held his breath.

Rodriguez tilted his head and stared at Jake through the glass as the guard moved forward to take him away. "I tell you this only because I am sorry that this girl suffered. Have you been protecting her?"

Jake nodded.

"Marquesa knew of her father. Victor Marquesa. But if he is hunting the daughter and knows you are not there, then I can only tell you that it is probably too late. He is a man without morals, without honor. He enjoys toying with his prey. He would kill to steal a cup of coffee from a blind man, and he would have no second thoughts."

TWENTY

The black SUV was still behind her.

Emma looked in her rearview mirror for the third time, then stepped on the gas as much as she dared.

With the freezing rain that had started yesterday before noon, she'd delayed her departure by one day, wanting to play it safe.

Now she wished she'd left yesterday.

Jake had once said that the Greyhound bus stop was thirty miles away, but he hadn't mentioned that the highway between False Lake and Masonville was a narrow, two-lane highway winding through steep foothills, or that the highway skirted numerous precipitous drop-offs marked only by a single guardrail. Sections of the road were still ice-covered and treacherous.

Was that SUV closer, now?

Emma began to pray as she negotiated a steep incline, then discovered a series of hairpin turns going down the other side. Wherever the road was shaded by tall pines, it was still glazed with ice. As she descended, she caught sight of the other SUV fishtailing on a tight corner, narrowly missing a series of boulders on the side of the road.

She jerked her attention back to the road, thankful that Oliver had loaned her his silver SUV for the trip. A ranch pickup wouldn't have made it up the first slippery hill.

Her palms were sweating inside her gloves and she tossed the gloves aside. Her heart started thumping against her ribs. There were no other cars on the road. She hadn't passed a single ranch or even a house since leaving False Lake. What would she do, clear out here and all alone, if someone ran her off the road?

The other SUV was gaining on her, and now she could see the outline of the driver's broad shoulders. The moment she hit a straight stretch of highway he sped up and rocketed to her rear bumper. Tapped it. Then he fell back. Floored his accelerator, and smashed into her bumper full force.

She felt her vehicle go weightless, then it hit the asphalt and swayed wildly. Tipping sideways on two wheels for one heart-stopping moment, it righted itself. Slammed back down on all four wheels. Then careened toward the side of the road.

Everything seemed to move in slow motion as her car arced out into space… and even her own scream seemed to go on and on, from some distance place. And then everything went dark.

Jake called the ranch landline during his rush to the airport but got only the answering machine. Oliver's cell phone was apparently turned off, because the call rolled right into his answering machine. He left messages on both, then fidgeted during the two-and-a-half hour flight to Billings. As soon as the plane landed, he raced through the airport to his truck and drove straight to the ranch.

The closer he got, the icier the roads were and the slower he could drive. At the ranch, he parked at the barns when he saw Oliver and Lane were doing chores.

He climbed out of the truck and skidded on the ice before catching his balance.

"Where is Emma?" he shouted. "Is she here?"

Oliver ambled over to the fence. "She left this morning."

Jake's heart sank. "I tried calling to make sure she stayed. No one answered."

"I was probably outside. Our land lines are still down, but at least we've got our electricity and cell phone service back."

"Where did she go—and how did she get there?"

"She went to Masonville to catch the 4:45 bus. I couldn't talk her out of it and with the storm brewing I couldn't leave the livestock, so I finally let her borrow my SUV. I figured it was safer."

"Have you heard from her since? Did you tell her to call when she got there?"

Looking at his watch, Oliver shook his head. "She was in a hurry, and she was flat determined to go. She should have gotten to Masonville long ago, and should be getting on the bus in less than an hour."

Jake spun on his heel and climbed back in his truck. He started the engine and rolled down his window. "Call the drugstore in Masonville and ask them if they see a woman who looks like her, and tell them to try to stop her from getting on that bus. Tell her...that there's an emergency, and I'm on the way. Then give me a call on my cell. Please."

"Got it."

"She could be in big, big trouble. Call the sheriff's department also. Tell them where she's headed."

"But—"

"Just do it." Jake backed the truck into a fast three-point turn, pulled up at the house to grab a rifle and a handgun, then he peeled out of the drive, kicking up a rooster tail of gravel and snow.

He had a bad, bad premonition about this.

The old man on death row had had nothing to gain or lose by lying, and after all the intervening hours since their conversation, his matter-of-fact words still had the power to chill Jake's blood.

If he is hunting the daughter, then I can only tell you that it is probably too late. He is a man without morals, without honor. He enjoys toying with his prey. He would kill to steal a cup of coffee from a blind man, and he would have no second thoughts.

* * *

Nausea crawled up Emma's throat. She felt dizzy and uncoordinated, with a pounding jungle beat throbbing in her head. She struggled to take another step in the thigh-high snow topped by a thick crust of ice, but every footstep felt as if she were pulling her feet out of hardening cement. And she was so tired. So very tired....

The man behind her cursed, shoved the barrel of his gun into her back and forced her on. She stumbled forward to her knees and her bare hands plunged through sharp fragments of ice, then deep into the snow beneath. Gloves. Did she have gloves?

She looked around wondering where they were. Were they red? Purple? They were pretty, with sparkles—

"Move it," the man snarled. "Unless you want to enjoy this place for all eternity."

That sounded bad. She blinked, struggling to force herself past the fogginess in her head. "Wh-why are you here?"

"Don't play stupid with me, sis. Your dad didn't cooperate, but I know you're smart enough to tell me exactly what I need to know. Got it?"

She faltered to a stop. "What?"

The man swore. "The investments. All of the accounts he handled for Rodriguez. It's all out there, just waiting."

"Accounts? *Rodriguez?* This is a mistake. I don't know—"

She didn't see the blow coming until his fist connected with her cheek. Her head snapped back. An explosion of pain and brilliant stars rocketed through her brain.

"Your dad knew. He always knew. I counted the minutes in prison, waiting, but then he was too stupid to make the right choice. Hand over the information, or die. He chose to die. Now it's your choice—because only you and he were left. He would have told you about the money."

What money?

It was a question she didn't dare ask.

She'd already been terrified. Now her fear ratcheted upward a hundredfold. This was her dad's killer. He was after information she didn't have. And when he learned the truth, her own life would end.

The man shoved her up the steep embankment and she half crawled, half fell on the way to the top. Her hands were bleeding and raw now, leaving crimson smears in the snow, though she could no longer feel them.

Through the dense trees in the ravine she could see soft glimmers of pink coming through the top branches at a long, low angle. The setting sun. That was west, then. But where was she—and how did she get here? How long had she been down here, unconscious? She trudged on, stumbling and falling. Grabbing at rough tree trunks with her cold, numb hands.

And then she remembered.

The black SUV following her too close. *Closer.* Ramming her own vehicle to send it off the road. The man behind her was probably the one who had been after her all along.

A crazy bubble of laughter threatened to work its way up her throat. Jake had tried to teach her how to protect herself with a gun. He'd worked with her on using the four-wheelers and the horses. He'd even showed her some powerful self-defense moves.

But he'd never guessed that she might end up at the mercy of a madman simply because he'd been able to run her off the road.

She gained the top edge of the embankment and found herself twenty feet from the black SUV, its motor still running. And she had nothing to lose.

She stumbled forward. Clawed up double handfuls of gravel and snow. Then spun around and threw them in her attacker's face with every ounce of her strength.

He jerked backward, staggered, trying to catch his balance on the steep slope— and gave her a split second of perfect opportunity. When she slammed a boot into his knee, he buckled....

Then he screamed and disappeared over the edge.

Jake pounded the steering wheel, wishing he dared go faster. The sun was dropping behind the mountains. All too soon it would be dark. Oliver had called twice—first to say that no one at the drugstore had seen someone with Emma's description and later, to say that she definitely hadn't gotten on the bus.

So where was she?

He'd pulled over three times when he'd seen damaged sections of guardrail along the highway. Each time, he prayed that he wouldn't see Oliver's SUV at the bottom of a ravine. So far, so good. But that still didn't mean she was safe.

The terrain was more rugged now, within the last ten miles to Masonville. Jake slowed, straining to see any tracks going off the side of the road. And then, out of the deepening gloom ahead, he could see another section of damaged guardrail that was crumpled and torn away like foil, its raw edges pointed out over a ravine. Fresh tire tracks left the road at that point.

A small inner voice whispered in his ear, warning him of danger as he eased his SUV into reverse and backed around the corner, out of sight. He climbed out, shoved his Beretta into the back waistband of his jeans and crept forward, staying close to the dark shadows at the side of the road.

He peered over the edge and felt his heart lodge in his throat. Oliver's SUV lay on its side at the bottom of a steep drop, caught sideways against a stand of birch.

Please, Lord, let her be safe.

There was one set of tracks in the snow leading down, though. Two sets coming back up—with a flattened area near the top, where there might have been an altercation—or possibly, rescuers dealing with injuries before continuing their ascent? Had they been struggling to make it up the hill with a stretcher?

He started down, slipping and sliding on the ice crusted snow, his heart pounding and a dozen scenarios rushing through his thoughts.

The SUV was empty, save for Emma's familiar leather purse and a duffel bag in the backseat. Odd—because a rescue team would've at least nabbed the purse for identification and insurance documentation. Had a passerby stopped to help?

The other possibility chilled Jake's blood.

If Marquesa had found her, perhaps even ran her off the road, he didn't even want to think about that outcome. Where would he take her? What would he do to force her to divulge information that she didn't even have?

Jake retrieved the purse and found Emma's cell phone on the floor of the car—another bad revelation. Wherever she was, she'd have no chance to call for help.

Back up on the highway he checked the reception bars on his cell phone and called 9-1-1.

"I've come up on a car in the ditch, ten miles west of Masonville," he barked into the phone. "Mile marker 23. I need to know if this was reported, or if the driver was taken to the hospital. Emma White."

"Hold on." The dispatcher fell silent, then came back on the line a couple minutes later. "No accidents reported. No emergency rescue vehicles have been called to that area. No new accident victims have been checked into the E.R. We did send a patrol car to that vicinity—a driver reported that someone flagged him down and begged for a ride to town, then he forced him out of his minivan and stole it."

"No one was with him? Not a young woman?"

"No, sir. But the odd thing was that

the carjacker appeared to be injured, but didn't head for town, where he could seek medical help or at least pick up one of the two highways that could take him across the state. The owner of the car said he turned around and went the other way. He headed toward a remote area of the mountains—and into the ice storm. My guess is that he won't get very far."

Good news, in that Emma wasn't with him. Better, that he'd needed a car. Which meant that she'd apparently managed to commandeer Marquesa's vehicle and escape—at least for now. And if she'd gone west she was probably heading back to the ranch.

Jake's momentary flash of relief dissipated as quickly as it had come.

She might have escaped, but she had a professional killer on her tail with a burning need to find her. So losing her temporary freedom—and then her life—might be just a matter of time.

TWENTY-ONE

An ice storm. A madman with crazy claims about her father. She'd been grabbed and threatened and somehow, she'd managed to escape. And now she'd just stolen an SUV.

Emma eyed the semiautomatic laying on the seat next to her, wondering if she could ever use such a weapon against another human being, then riveted her attention on the icy road ahead.

There'd been a reason Jake had taken her out for target practice. If it meant her life, or the lives of people she loved, she could. She definitely could.

But had she made the right choice in going back to the ranch?

Heading for an unknown, small town where she didn't know a soul, where she might not be able to locate a sheriff's office—if there even was one in town—in time had seemed like a far greater risk. She could hardly keep going across the state in a borrowed vehicle, and the idea of getting on that bus was ludicrous now. She'd be a sitting duck the minute she got on board.

Once she got to the ranch she could call 9-1-1 and then hope that her attacker was still at the bottom of that ravine close to town, where a deputy could go pick him up and arrest him before he froze to death.

Her breath caught as the SUV skidded sideways on a patch of black ice, then its wheels gained traction, launching the vehicle forward. She eased back on the accelerator and turned up the long lane leading to the Rocking K. *Safe at last.*

* * *

Victor impatiently reprogrammed the dashboard GPS of the minivan he'd confiscated, then muttered a curse. Outdated, useless piece of technology that it was, it still wanted to send him to Billings instead of the Kincaid ranch, but in the process of making false turns he'd found a shortcut and might even beat Emma there.

Her destination was no guess—he'd heard the sound of his SUV heading away from Masonville. She probably thought she would be safe at Kincaid's ranch with two rifle-toting cowboys to protect her. But she had no idea what she was up against. He was through playing games and he was through with being cautious.

And once those cowboys were dead and out of the way, she was going to find that out, then give him exactly what he wanted.

The front door at the ranch was unlocked as usual, the house appearing dark and empty. "Oliver? Lane?" Emma called out as she turned on lights in the kitchen and living room. "Anyone home?"

No one answered.

A frisson of uneasiness crawled up her spine as she checked the office and bedrooms, then went back to the kitchen and peered out the windows toward the barn. Swirls of sleet and snow danced under the security lights, obliterating the view of the barns. Were Lane and Oliver out there doing chores?

No one knew she was coming back. Had they all left for the night? Surely not in this weather. Zipping her jacket up once again, she stepped outside and hurried to the barn. Icy needles pricked at her skin and the wind snaked up her waist-length jacket, bringing with it the damp chill of snow.

On the way to the barn she found Oliver's truck parked near the house and, much farther away in the shadows, an unfamiliar gray minivan. Maisie arose from her dog bed in the tack room and licked

Emma's hand, then went back and curled up to go to sleep again. "Where is everyone, old girl?"

Grabbing a rifle from the case in the tack room, she chambered a round and pocketed extra ammunition.

Leaving the door ajar, she stepped out into the aisle and tiptoed past Gilbert the Goose's favorite haunt—an empty stall by the tack room used for pitchforks, shovels and wheelbarrows—calling for Oliver and Lane as she moved down the aisle and glanced in the stalls. She opened the door to the indoor arena. The lights were off, so maybe the men were out haying the cattle or moving livestock to safer pastures because of the weather...but in the *dark?*

She shut the door and turned back toward the front of the barn. Her heart lifted at the sight of a tall figure standing just inside the double doors at the end of the aisle. "Oliver?"

"Not even close."

The all too familiar voice was low, filled

with anger. He stepped forward into the light and she now saw the gun held in his raised hands, pointed straight at her.

"Put the rifle down. Nice and steady."

She wobbled. Moved a slow step back, then another.

"I'm telling you, put that rifle down," he snarled. "You couldn't lift that barrel up an inch and I would have you dead on the floor."

Farther...come farther. She held the rifle out at her side and eased another two steps back.

"What, are you deaf? *Put the rifle down.*" He moved down the aisle toward her, and now she could see his face was ruddy with anger. "You can't run. You can't hide. You have no options. Understand?"

"Who are you? What do you want? I don't have any money, if that's what you're after." She stepped back another yard and made a show of turning to lean the rifle against the front of a stall a few more feet behind her.

"Oh. I think you do." The man gave her a cocky stare as he moved toward her, his gun still raised. "And now that your father is dead, you're going to tell me exactly how to find it."

She held her breath and prayed that Gilbert was paying attention to the interloper in his territory. She raised her voice. "What?"

"I said, you're going to—"

An explosion of white feathers, squawks and wide, beating wings erupted from Gilbert's lair, his serpentlike neck snaking straight for the side of the man's face.

"Hey!" He stumbled sideways just as Maisie burst out of the tack room from the opposite side, barking furiously and snapping at his heels.

His gun hand swung wildly as he tried to kick away the dog and fend off the furious goose. The gun fired into the air, the deafening sound echoing like a cannon shot in the metal building.

The goose rose on its powerful wings and nailed the side of Marquesa's neck and as he fought it off, handfuls of feathers flying, Maisie sank her teeth into his calf. He screamed, staggered against the front of a stall, where the startled horse inside spun around and blasted the stall front with both back hooves, the ringing of iron against steel adding to the melee.

Marquesa screamed. The gun fell and skittered away across the cement.

The furious bird flapped away, still hissing. Disgruntled, Maisie still held the man at bay, her teeth bared and the hair along her spine raised. Marquesa looked around wildly for the gun.

"Don't move," Emma said quietly. She lifted the rifle and took aim at Marquesa's chest, shaking inwardly, though Jake's lessons came back to her crystal clear.

"As if," Marquesa snarled. "No little

suburban librarian like you could pull that trigger."

"Want to bet?" She sighted down the barrel. "I've been taking lessons. I've gotten quite good with the clay pigeons, and you aren't moving nearly that fast. And if I just aim for center mass I'm bound to hit something important. Right?"

He started to reach for his back waistband, and she'd seen enough movies to know that meant a second weapon.

"No...I want your hands up, where I can see them."

He stilled. "So what are you going to do, stand there forever and hold that rifle on me? You can't make a phone call and hold it steady. Sooner or later you'll just have to give up. Do you realize how rich you could be, if you cooperate? We'd both be millionaires...and then I'd just disappear. You'd never see me again."

"That's ridiculous. Keep those hands *up*."

"Your old man knew all about it—all of

the investments Rodriguez salted away before he was incarcerated. He didn't co-operate, either, and he's dead."

She blinked. "My father had nothing to do with that man."

"Why do you think you were there when that senator was murdered? Your father was sent there—it was supposed to be a meeting, not a murder—but someone got gun happy and it turned into a disaster."

"That's not true!"

"Isn't it? Only when a surveillance camera helped track your dad down did he agree to testify against the cartel. He chose being a snitch to ending up in prison himself…and he still knew all about the offshore accounts, so he did pretty well for himself."

She was trembling now. Deep shudder-ing waves worked through her. The rifle barrel wobbled. "You're lying."

"No. I'm banking on the fact that he would've told his only child how to access that money, to give her financial security for the rest of her life. Why do you think I'd bother with trying to track you down?"

He moved so fast, whipping out that gun at the small of his back, that she barely had time to react. She squeezed off a shot taking no time to aim.

His own gun fired a millisecond later and she felt something rip through the bulky insulation of her down jacket's shoulder.

He buckled against the wall, his eyes wide with shock, gripping his upper thigh with one hand. But the other hand still held his gun at his side.

"D-don't make me fire again," Emma warned, trying to control the tremble in her voice. "I'd rather shoot you than die myself, believe me. It's not much of a choice."

An exterior door squealed, footsteps rushed across the tack room, then the interior door swung open and crashed against the wall. *Jake.*

"And it wouldn't be one for me, either,"

he said coldly, confiscating Marquesa's weapon. "Especially not after what I found in the house."

Emma's heart lurched and she suddenly felt faint. "Oh, no—not Lane and Oliver."

Grabbing a length of bale twine hanging on the hay stall door, Jake tied Marquesa's hands tightly behind his back, then he shoved the man against the front of a stall and tied him to the iron bars so Marquesa couldn't move.

Jake took a step away and glared at the intruder. "There was *no reason* to rough up an old man and a teenager like that. *None.* But the one good thing from all this is that you are through. Forever."

"So you think," Marquesa spat.

"I know so. The sheriff is on his way, so take a good look around, because after this night you'll never be free again."

TWENTY-TWO

Emma nestled in Jake's arms, watching the EMTs strap Marquesa onto a gurney. A deputy rechecked his handcuffs, then they loaded him into the ambulance.

Another unit had left five minutes earlier with Lane and Oliver.

One of the deputies walked over to Emma. "Are you sure we can't take you in to the E.R.? From the looks of it you had quite a crash when you rolled your SUV, and dizziness can be a sign of a concussion. Looks like you've got cuts and bruises, too."

"I'm fine. I just want to stay here."

"I'm driving her to the E.R. right now," Jake said. "I'm not taking any chances."

"You are one fortunate woman, Ms. White. Do you have any idea who that guy was?"

"Some."

"Victor Marquesa already has a major rap sheet, and he's wanted in three states. Murder-for-hire charges from last year could well put him away with no chance of parole, *ever*. This will definitely seal the deal."

She shivered. "That would be a good thing."

"We've already got most of the details for my report, but I may need to call you tomorrow to clarify some things."

"Believe me, I'll do anything to make sure that man is put behind bars."

"Good." He looked over his shoulder. "I've got to follow the ambulance. See you at the hospital?"

Jake nodded and waited until the deputy climbed into his patrol car. Then he gently turned Emma to face him and cupped her face in his hand. "I can't believe how close I came to losing you tonight. A few minutes difference…"

"A few minutes difference, and I'd probably be dead. I would be, if you hadn't been so close by. I fired instinctively in reaction to Marquesa going for his gun, but I don't think I could have done it a second time."

Jake shook his head slowly in wonder. "You are amazing, Emma."

"It was purely an adrenaline surge. I was afraid he would shoot you, me, or both of us if you showed up here and he caught sight of you." She closed her eyes. "I feel so awful about what happened to Lane and Oliver."

"They'll be fine. A few bumps and bruises—probably a concussion when Marquesa hit Oliver over the head and knocked him out. I'm sure the docs will watch over him closely."

"It was all my fault. If I hadn't come here

in the first place, all of you would have been safe."

"But what would have become of you? This way, you had a chance. I think God was really looking out for you when he brought you to my trailer in Ogallala."

She felt so tired, so very tired, but managed a weak laugh at that. "Most of my life has been so dramatic, so fraught with danger, that I figured God didn't even have me on His radar anymore. I was sure He didn't care. But I think I prayed more in the past six hours than I ever have in my life, and there were so many ways I felt His guidance. It was like…I don't know, exactly. Like I had a father's arms around me with every move I made."

The weather cleared and the sun shone bright on the white, crystalline world at the ranch a few days later. Oliver and Lane were out feeding cattle before breakfast, and Jake had just come in from feeding the horses to find Emma cooking scrambled eggs and bacon.

After shucking off his winter coat, gloves and boots, he crossed the kitchen to hold her close and dropped a kiss on her forehead. "You've been so quiet lately that you have me worried. So what are your plans now? Please don't tell me that they involve Masonville and a bus ticket."

"No bus tickets just yet. I…um…didn't tell you the truth when I said I didn't like living here at your ranch. I love working here. I was just afraid that someone like Victor would show up and that some of you could die."

"But that's all over. The sheriff tells me that Marquesa has already been extradited to Chicago, and the feds are really eager to put him away for good." Jake grinned down at her. "But no matter what happens, I'm sure he'll never look at a librarian quite the same way again."

She looked up at him, her answering smile tinged with sadness. "I still have to leave, you know. I've got to retrieve my package in Deer Lodge, because I apparently have to pick it up in person after all. And now I need to try to find my sister. After all these years, the thought of seeing her again is just beyond comprehension. Maybe my life will even be normal, someday."

"You don't need to face that all alone, Emma."

"I don't expect you to leave this ranch and go off on an expedition like this. It might take weeks. Months. I never dared try to find her before because of the WITSEC rules. But I just can't give up until I find her—she's all the family I have left."

"It may not be that difficult." Jake tried to rein in his grin, then gave up. "How long will it take you to pack?"

Her eyes opened wide. "Ten minutes, max. Really—we could go today?"

"Yep. You can get that package and be done with those worries. But on the way home, there's one more stop we need to make."

"Sure—anything. I can just bring along a book and read in the truck."

"You won't want to be reading when we make this stop. I found your sister, Emma—or at least, my friendly P.I. did. He gave me her phone number and I called her last night."

Emma paled, her lips trembling. "You did? You really talked to her?"

"Kris had some troubles of her own over the years, which might have made it hard for you to find her. But now she's doing well, she's married to a rancher, and she lives outside of Battle Creek, Montana. She was ecstatic about seeing you again. All these years she's been searching for you, desperate for any news of where you'd gone."

"Oh, Jake." Her eyes shining, Emma reached up and drew him into a fierce embrace, then held his face between her hands and pulled him down for a kiss.

"Wow," he murmured.

"I can't thank you enough for everything you've done. You've given me my life back."

This time, he was the one to gently embrace her. He kissed her soft, sweet mouth, and in that moment, he felt more alive, more loved, than he ever had before.

"No decisions now—I don't want you to confuse gratitude with deeper feelings and then regret any decisions later." He cleared his throat, suddenly feeling awkward and inept. "And I know this seems sort of backward, since you've been living and working at the ranch awhile already. But I really care about you, Emma. I think I've already fallen in love with you. After we take care of getting to Deer Lodge and meeting your sister, I really hope you'll come back here to stay."

She grinned, reached up and pulled him down for another sweet kiss. "My feelings exactly, cowboy. Because there's no place on earth that I'd rather be."

* * * * *

Dear Reader,

Thank you for joining Emma on her journey from secrecy and fear, to freedom and a love of a lifetime in *Duty to Protect*. I've often wondered what it would be like to give up everything one had of their current life—and then essentially have to live a lie just to survive. For Emma, her flight led her to a kind protective man and new beginnings, which were the answer to her prayers.

I love to hear from readers. You can find me at my website, www.roxannerustand.com, my blog, at http://roxannerustand.blogspot.com, or at PO Box 2550, Cedar Rapids, Iowa 52406. I also have a new e-newsletter, and all subscribers have a chance at quarterly drawings for autographed books and other prizes. You can sign up with a simple click of a button at my website.

Blessings to you all,

Roxanne

Questions for Discussion

1. Emma has lived her life essentially as a lie—with varying names and locations meant to keep her and her family safe. In this story she discovers she can no longer trust the system that has been protecting her, and she has to strike out on her own. Although few of us will ever need the shelter of a witness protection program, big changes in one's life can also be very unsettling. Have you ever had to face a frightening or surprising situation that changed the course of your life? How did you cope? How did it change you?

2. Of all the places and moments in time, Emma finds herself at a truckstop at the same time as Jake Kincaid, and she manages to hide in his trailer to escape her pursuer. He becomes her protector. In real life, we sometimes encounter circumstances that end up being per-

fect for our needs in some way. Do you think these situations are an answer to prayer, or just a coincidence?

3. Emma is on the run and tells Jake some lies to protect her true identity. Are lies ever justified? What about the social "white lies" that so many people tell?

4. Jake was a sheriff's deputy in Wyoming for ten years. One of the situations that made him leave the force was his mounting guilt and frustration over a serial rapist case that the department struggled to solve. Despite long hours and every effort to identify and catch the suspect, the man remained on the loose and attacked even more women before he was finally captured. Jake still feels he failed those women. Are there any situations in your life in which you feel guilt or frustration because you weren't able to help someone, or wish you could have done

something differently? How can one deal with those feelings?

5. Jake went to visit Eduardo Rodriguez in prison to try to ferret out the truth about the man pursuing Emma. Do you think Eduardo spoke the truth? Why, or why not?

6. Emma prays throughout her daily life. An example is at the end of Chapter 15. How often do you pray? Is it part of your own daily life, or do you pray mostly at more formal moments—say, at church and before meals?

7. Discuss some of the ways your prayers have been answered over the years. Have your prayers been answered in greater ways than you expected? Or in ways you didn't expect?

8. Emma wounds Marquesa at the end of the book. How far would you be

able to go to defend yourself and your loved ones?

9. Marquesa threatened Emma's life. Do you think she should forgive him? Are there people in your life who have hurt you badly? Have you been able to forgive them?

10. As the leader of a drug cartel and a man responsible for the deaths of many people over the years, do you think Rodriguez can be forgiven by God?

11. What are the ways in which Jake is a true hero in this story? Who are some of the everyday heroes in your own life or your community, and why?

12. When Jake's wife, Maura, left him, he was devastated. He'd grown up with loving parents in a solid relationship, and he wanted that life for himself, as well. Are there circumstances when divorce is the only option?

13. Ed Feezer was a trusted employee who helped steal cattle from Jake's ranch. Have you ever been betrayed by someone you trusted? How did you feel? How did you handle the situation?

14. Discuss the following Bible verse, and what it means in your own daily life: *Don't worry about anything; instead, pray about everything. Tell God what you need, and thank him for what he has done. If you do this, you will experience God's peace, which is far more wonderful than the human mind can understand. His peace will guard your hearts and minds as you live in Christ Jesus. Philippians 4:6-7.*

15. By the end of the story, Jake and Emma have found in each the perfect qualities for a happy-ever-after ending. What five qualities do you think are the most important for a loving and enduring relationship?